THE SUPERLATIVE MAN

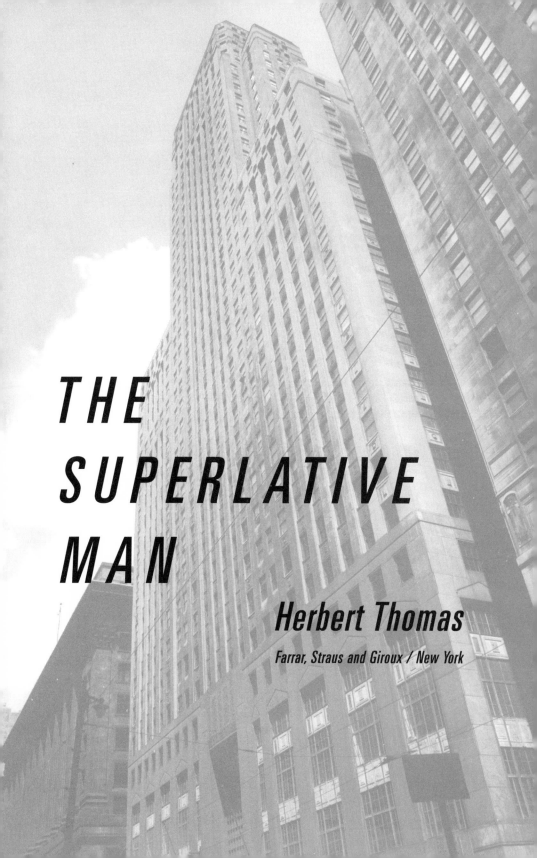

THE
SUPERLATIVE
MAN

Herbert Thomas

Farrar, Straus and Giroux / New York

Farrar, Straus and Giroux
19 Union Square West
New York 10003

Published simultaneously in Canada by HarperCollins*CanadaLtd*
Printed in the United States of America
Designed by Jonathan D. Lippincott
First edition, 1997

Library of Congress Cataloging-in-Publication Data
Thomas, Herbert, 1957–
    The superlative man / Herbert Thomas. — 1st ed.
        p.   cm.
    ISBN 0-374-27209-3 (alk. paper)
    I. Title.
PS3570.H5628S8   1997
813'.54—dc21   97-268

If heroism becomes chronic, it ends in a cramp, and the cramp leads to catastrophe or neurosis or both.

Carl Jung

THE
SUPERLATIVE
MAN

The Accident

Red and white lights splashed ahead in the darkness. Harvey Gander pulled over to wait beside the guardrail, a stretch of squat barrier posts strung with sagging cable. Two headlights rounded a curve, and a white ambulance van slowed at the sight of him, eased its way between the flank of his car and the base of the cliff, the ambulance so close he could reach through his open window and touch it. It reappeared in his rearview mirror, the red bulb swirling atop the white cab, a silent siren.

Gander pressed the accelerator pedal and his car drifted away from the rail, rounded the bend, the cliff sliding away and the tiny scene by the river's edge opening before him: a few scattered cars on a smooth dirt bank by the water and, beyond them, a tiny flock of shadows, a cluster of men gathered below the rocks.

Gander's headlights swung across them, faces turning in the glare, his lights drifting past and out across the black river, hovering there, and then dying as he cut his engine. He popped the door handle and sat bathed in the dirty yellow light of his car's interior.

He leaned against the trunk of his car. A hundred feet away, the men stood with their faces turned toward him, pale under dark hats. Beyond them, in the crumpled landscape of an ancient rock slide, a car's twisted silver wreckage lay wedged in the rocks, flattened and battered, one door sprung at a crooked angle like a clipped wing.

One of the men was approaching, his slow gait a familiar signature in the shadows. "Gander," he said, his face materializing under the hat brim, a hand reaching out to Gander's shoulder, "you got my message."

"I was out of the office. It was there when I got back."

"I should have told you in person."

"It's okay, Martin."

The hand withdrew from his shoulder, the two men face-to-face.

"It was already dark?" Gander asked.

"Yeah, it was dark. They were up there on Route 12." The head nodding to the high edge of the cliff, a wall of black shadow rising a hundred and fifty feet. "You know the road?"

Gander nodded.

"They were headed north when out of nowhere he came over the hill and flew in front of their windshield. Never even saw them, just flew out over the cliff on his way down to the Great Bridge."

Gander looked back over his shoulder. Far down the river the Great Bridge spanned the night, a formidable silhouette rising like a gateway to a twinkling constellation of city lights.

Gander asked, "Why was he flying so low to the ground?"

"Nobody knows. But the word is he was on his way to save some kid who was ready to jump from the bridge."

"Did he?"

"Jump? No. He got there in time, flew way up to the very top of the bridge and talked him down. But back here it was all over. When he cut across their windshield, they lost control and went through the rail. The medics said they died on impact. They didn't suffer, Gander."

"Once they'd landed."

"Yeah, once they'd landed."

"That was them in the ambulance?"

Martin nodded. He stepped over to the car to stand beside Gander, leaning against the car's trunk, their shoulders almost touching. "Why don't you let me give you a lift back?" he said. "One of the other guys can bring your car."

"Who's over there?"

"Cops and reporters."

"Any of ours?"

"Elmo Jade's there. He's writing it up. You want me to talk to him?"

"Yeah. Tell him to write it small and bury it in the back. I don't want a big story. This is going to take a while to sink in."

"I'll ask him."

"I'd appreciate it. And thanks, but I'll head back myself."

"Up to you."

But Gander waited, his hand on the door handle, Martin leaning against the trunk, arms folded across his chest and his face sideways, watching him.

"I'm glad he saved the kid," Gander said to his car.

"Yeah, the boy's okay," Martin answered.

"It's funny, you know."

"I know," Martin nodded. "I know. Don't say it."

"But it's true."

"Yes, I know. Don't say it. I know."

"The Superlative Man killed my parents."

The burial ceremony was three days later, in a small cemetery at the north end of the city, an old sheep meadow where the sheep had given gradual way to the dead and repeating rows of tiny headstones marched in drab uniform against the city, which surrounded the field on all sides now and peered in from rowhouse windows over the lip of bordering trees. Harvey Gander glanced at the faces of the other mourners, gathered around the two graves in a near-perfect circle to pay their respects, their faces framed by black hats and black jackets and pale against the flat gray sky. Their faces looked strung together like some otherworldly charm bracelet.

A representative from the Department of Public Health had been asked to officiate at the small ceremony. He coughed politely and twenty-five pairs of eyes turned to him.

"Good afternoon," he said, "and thank you for coming. It looks like we'll beat the rain after all." The man smiled broadly at everyone and at no one in particular. Gander's eyes drifted back to the open graves.

"I am Ray Teller," the man continued, "and I've been invited to do the afternoon's reading." He waited, looking intently, even expectantly, about the circle, as though hoping someone might speak up in reply. Hearing nothing, he looked down to the small black book in his hand, about to read.

Gander interrupted quietly. "Thank you, Ray," he said.

Ray Teller looked up and an appreciative smile flickered across his smooth, almost featureless face. He folded the black book against his shirtfront and spoke to Gander directly.

"You know, Harvey?" he said. "Even though I didn't know your parents personally—I mean, I never met them in my life—I feel connected somehow to your pain. Not because your parents are such a great loss—I'm sure they're a great loss but that's not what I mean—but because I feel a sort of sympathy for your predicament. The way they died was so . . . *unusual*." Ray looked about the faces of the other mourners with renewed interest, raised his book, and commenced to read, enunciating his words, pausing where appropriate for effect, his eyes lifting to one mourner or another for emphasis.

The ceremony flowed along toward an uneventful close, Ray darting an occasional, meaningful glance at Gander, when a sudden rustle of whispers around the circle grew in intensity and caused Ray to break off his reading and look up. His eyes widened in alarm. Gander turned to see. Across the open graves, partially hidden between the shoulders of two mourners, the Superlative Man stared back, the ivory-colored *S* and *M* emblazoned across his chest, his eyes clear and piercing. Gander felt the gaze sink deep within. An electric charge skated behind his face. The Superlative Man lowered his eyes to the earth.

Gander's breath came short and rapid. He could not get the air deep enough into his lungs and turned to Ray, who stood open-mouthed, the black book open in his palm, his right forefinger still marking his place. All around the grave the mourners stared at the Superlative Man.

In that small moment of shock, Ray saw his opportunity. He folded the book closed at his waist. "O, brothers and sisters," he intoned.

Eyebrows raised and faces turned slowly to Ray, who stood waiting with one hand lifted. He said, "We are gathered here today to mourn the passing of Joseph and Elizabeth Gander, a man and a woman we admired for the lives they led and for the lives they touched. We knew them, we loved them, and we will miss them."

Around the circle the mourners watched Ray, transfixed and appalled by this naked attempt to impress the most recent arrival. The Superlative Man stared stone-faced at the ground.

"But why?" Ray inquired. "Why are we here? Better to ask, Why are they gone? Joseph and Elizabeth's accident was a crazy mishap, a one-in-a-million fluke. Picture this: the Superlative Man flying close to the ground. Then Joe and Liz Gander, a couple of regular folks on their way home at night in their car. When all of a sudden, whoosh! and it was over. I ask you, is anyone to *blame* for this tragedy? Friends, here today we must accept what's happened for what it is: a monstrous accident. And so we gather to pay our respects, to remember, and then to go home and try and forget."

Ray bowed slightly, then looked up expectantly at the Superlative Man, who stared fiercely back. Abruptly the Superlative Man turned and walked along the outer perimeter of the circle toward Harvey Gander.

Gander stepped out of the circle to meet him.

Never before had he stood this close. With the scarlet-and-ivory cloth spread tightly across his chest and the scarlet cape hanging loosely behind, the Superlative Man was the most perfectly formed human being Gander had ever laid eyes on. The face was a sculptor's dream, an idea of a perfect statue, some great work carved from the heart of marbled stone. His countenance hummed with intelligence and power, in the blue eyes, in the black hair pouring smoothly back from the face, in the quiet control of the lips, drawn slightly down at the corners, suggesting sorrow, perhaps remorse. His very posture spoke to Gander: the sloping shoulders and long arms falling into fists at his sides, the red-stockinged feet pressed slightly apart, a body coiled for flight yet motionless and silent, perhaps seeking forgiveness.

"I don't know what to say to you," the Superlative Man said at last.

Gander would never know what possessed him. The words were simply there, spilling out before he was conscious of their meaning. He said, "As long as I live, I hope I never see your face again."

The Superlative Man's blue eyes closed briefly, but with barely a missed beat he answered back, "You get one thing straight, Gander. Your old man drove off that cliff, not me."

As the Superlative Man turned and walked down the gravel path toward the bordering trees, Gander looked in panic to the other mourners, none of whom had moved, all of whom stared back at him as though he'd been conceived in one of the open graves. Stunned and horrified by what he had done, Gander grinned at them as wildly, as brilliantly, as his face could manage.

Harvey Gander

Harvey Gander stood before a newsstand's colorful display, scanning the collage of headlines and faces with an experienced eye, first spotting his own newspaper, the *Metropolitan Meteor*, and absorbing at a glance the front page of the *Daily Mercury*, before taking in the hundred and more dailies, weeklies, and monthlies; the specials, annuals, and perennials that grew in bright splashes of color, and threatened to engulf the little newsstand man whose bespectacled face, in its modest window, looked like just another front page. It took Gander a moment to see him.

His was the face whose mouth was moving.

"Wha'd'ya want?" it requested.

"Pack of Fortunes."

"Right," the man said and slid the cigarettes across a narrow counter. Gander slid back a nickel and a dime, took the cigarettes and, thanking the man with a nod, opened the packet as he walked over to a wire wastebasket sitting by the curb to the side of the stand.

He peered into the wastebasket.

Staring back up at him, from a color-cover monthly nestled in the lunchtime debris, was a blowup, a full-figure photograph of the

Superlative Man. Gander analyzed the grainy exposure: a distant shot, a bit overblown, but still something of a coup. Not many could boast a photograph like this, and color at that. Most editors had to settle for an artist's rendering, awful caricatures meant to capture some marketing editor's notion of the mood of the city, pictures they commissioned and then splayed across covers to boost sales. He leaned down and reached into the wastebasket, turned back the cover to a first-page, large-type editorial, and read:

> You hold history in your hands. Magazine history, at any rate.
>
> We thought last month was good. 291,000 copies: a new record and one we were proud to boast of. Then came this photograph. The moment we saw it we knew it was a cover. The moment we saw it we ordered a run of 500,000 copies. *Half a million.* And at press time, even as we write, with advance orders we're *sold out.* We've ordered a quarter-million more. Hats off to Barney Coppers, one of our unmatchable crew of staff photographers.
>
> The photograph: one of the greatest face shots of the Superlative Man we've ever seen. Ever. But not just a face shot. The Superlative Man landing after a lightning-fast descent, one foot down, his cape high behind him, arms up. Poised for balance. Ready to strike.
>
> This photograph captures in one shining moment the glory of the Superlative Man's greatest season. Nearly a year of heart-stopping rescues. And during the past few months a series of double rescues that can only be called spectacular. Runaway trains, raging fires, children screaming to be saved. How many people walk this city alive today because of this peerless hero? How do we feel about this ongoing miracle? We think the demand for this issue says it all.

· · ·

Gander flipped back the cover for another look. Who could blame them for honking their horn? It *was* a good shot, the kind that makes a photographer's career. He tore the cover away and folded the picture into his inner breast pocket, chucked his unlit cigarette into the gutter and headed down the sidewalk.

Born and raised in the city, Harvey Gander did not believe himself to have acquired much more of a life history than that. But those fragments of a story line that had accumulated ended abruptly with his parents' accident. Over a year had passed since their deaths, but in so many ways he still hadn't absorbed the loss, hadn't yet registered the implications.

The never-ending stream of attention poured daily onto the Superlative Man only made it worse, for Gander lived in a city that saw in this superhero the realization of an American dream, in which fear and danger and death had an antidote, good was more knowing than evil, and accidents almost but never quite happened because lives were saved, victims healed, mothers and children reunited. Gander wanted in his heart to believe, and had believed as a child, but felt recently as though he'd somehow lost his citizenship in the city he had always called home. He'd spent the year since his parents' accident wandering in a kind of self-effacing haze.

A taxicab skated close to the curb, the driver honking and pointing at a man next to Gander on the sidewalk. Apparently the man had been about to step out into a gap in traffic, and he shook his fist wildly at the cab, already angling away across the street to the curb opposite, where a second man stood beckoning.

Gander waited on the corner for the light to change. Halfway up the next block, a movie marquee jutted out over the sidewalk announcing the latest feature, *Easy Street*. He decided to slip away for an hour or two before heading back to the office.

He'd seen the show the week before. It was about a private eye who gets an unsigned letter and five new one-hundred-dollar bills in the mail. The letter gives him the lowdown on a smuggling conspiracy and asks if he'd investigate. He takes the job, blows the lid off the conspiracy, and along the way acts the wise guy with a girl who starts out bad but grows to love him.

Under the marquee four double-glass doors stood flush with the sidewalk. Just inside, in a narrow outer lobby, a ticket seller sat propped in a glass booth. She was a middle-aged blonde wearing butterfly glasses with sparkling wings and a tiny silver chain that swung down from her temples and around the back of her neck.

"One?" she said.

Gander nodded. Her makeup was cake-deep under the glare of the overhead fixture, a cut-glass globe etched with chubby angels and bunches of grapes. White face powder dusted the shoulders of her navy-blue jacket, and layers of cream-colored blouse sprouted under her chin like a cauliflower.

"Forty cents," she requested.

Gander reached into his pocket for a handful of change and with his thumb slid a nickel, a quarter, and a dime onto the counter. The woman tore a ticket from a coiled roll and held it out the little window.

"Cartoon's just starting," she said.

Gander nodded and walked through a red-curtained door. Inside, the main lobby was all scarlet and gold, not just in the plush red carpet with gold swirls that ran along the candy counter and up the balcony stairways on either side, but in the phony gold columns rising to the ceiling and the blood-red wallpaper, too.

A kid in a purple monkey suit with matching fez and gold tassel reached for Gander's ticket. The kid said, "Yessir, cartoon's just gettin' started."

"No rush," Gander said. "I saw it last week. It was kinda silly."

"It's a good cartoon," the kid stated. He had flat green eyes and small teeth. Under his ear a petal-shaped scar trailed down his neck. He dropped the ticket into a slot in the ticket box beside him, patted the lid twice, and said to Gander, "And it already started."

Gander took the left-side stairway to the balcony. At the top, just inside the heavy curtain, he waited for his eyes to adjust. Beside him in the dark, another kid in a monkey suit watched the cartoon. On the screen a mouse with droopy ears and a paunchy belly scurried around a corner but skidded on its heels at the sight of a giant cat's head with a gaping mouth and a tongue rolled out like a red carpet.

Down the steps to the left, three rows back from the rail and three seats in from the aisle, a brunette sat in profile, eating popcorn. The silver light wore her features smooth, like moonlight. She was all black and white like a movie actress. Gander slipped into the aisle seat at the end of her row, and she glanced over. She had high cheekbones and a pointy chin. Her eyes were dark and shiny. Gander whispered, "Hello there." Without a glimmer of a reply she turned back to the screen and resumed eating her popcorn, a kernel at a time.

The cartoon ended with a picture of the cat all dressed up like a suckling pig, an apple crammed into its mouth, and a circle of mice in grass skirts and leis doing a hula dance around it. Gander peeked over at the woman. She tugged at her lapels and pulled her jacket closer about her shoulders.

A brass fanfare burst forth from the overhead speakers, the words *NEWS OF AMERICA* marching in bold white type across the screen. The heavy brass faded to a Morse code tap-tap-tapping under an announcer's rising voice.

"All across America, in homes and in the streets, in the cities and out in the great farmlands, NEWS OF AMERICA is there as it happens."

Gander knew what was coming and dreaded it. For weeks now

the newsreels had been devoted to the Superlative Man and his most recent exploits, a sensational string of double rescues. He hated the hype, the fawning adulation, but here he was, sitting through it all over again. He wondered if some part of him didn't want to watch.

"The time: almost midnight. The day? Call it mid-July. The night is hot. The city swelters. Above the streets an office girl looks out her apartment window, watching the sky for rain. Down in the street a copper walks his beat, his tie loose and his sleeves rolled. It's against regulations, but his sergeant's too hot to enforce them. Out on the piers the hoboes sit on the river's edge, bare feet dangling over the water. A silent night in an urban inferno."

"When suddenly," Gander muttered at the screen, "the Superlative Man sprinkles crushed ice all over everybody."

The woman turned in place and stared.

"High on the eleventh floor of a modern apartment building, the frayed cord of an electric fan smolders. Sparks leap to a hanging curtain tassel and dance along the cloth."

"To the sound of Latin rhythms," Gander interjected.

"Shh!" the woman hissed.

"At her window a mother clutches her baby and screams for help. Meanwhile, on the other side of town, a ship's horn blows, the captain frantic on his bridge. Something has gone wrong as the ship heads dangerously toward the piers."

"Run for your lives, hoboes!" Gander warned.

"Will you please be *quiet?*" the woman insisted. Gander looked over at her. She sat hunched in her chair, clutching her popcorn to her breast.

"Sorry," Gander offered. "It's just so silly."

"What's so silly?" she ventured.

"I don't know. This foolishness about the Superlative Man."

"*What* foolishness?"

"*. . . flying with mother and child . . .*"

"They make you think the Superlative Man can save everybody, like he can save the whole country."

"... *steering the ship to safety, the happy mother waving gratefully from the pier.*"

"Look," Gander exclaimed to the newsreel, "he left the mother and her kid down on the pier with all the bums."

"Usher!" the woman called out. "Usher!"

The kid in the monkey suit crept down from the top of the stairs. "What is it, lady?" he said.

"This man is *bothering* me."

"Who, *him?*"

"He's trying to *talk* to me."

"Hey, mister, you gotta leave her alone or I'm gonna have to ask you to leave."

"... *stunning chain of double rescues ...*"

"I wasn't talking to her. I was talking to myself."

"Okay, so maybe you better move."

"It's this dopey newsreel," Gander answered. "You guys have been showing the same one for almost two weeks now."

"It's a good newsreel."

"Yeah, like the cartoon."

"It's a good cartoon."

"Good my ass."

"All right, buddy. You're outta here."

"... *the office girl asleep in her bed. The copper on his beat, his tie neatly knotted and his cuffs buttoned ...*"

By the curtain at the top of the stairs, Gander looked back down at the screen, the silhouette of the usher standing in the aisle, the woman with the silver face eating her popcorn.

"... *and the lonesome hoboes sit at the river's edge, their feet dangling over the water as they stare at the harbor and the sea beyond.*"

Brass fanfare.

The Assignment

When he was eighteen years old, Harvey Gander took a job as a messenger for the *Metropolitan Meteor*. From the messenger pool he was eventually promoted into the mail room, and one morning as he sorted envelopes, an old-time reporter by the name of Martin Gale walked by and stopped to chat. Still drunk from the night before, Martin waxed sentimental. By the time he was through, he'd plucked out Gander as a junior features reporter.

Martin Gale had been a reporter for longer than Gander had been alive, floating from one job to the next when each paper in turn got fed up with his drinking and sent him packing. At which point he'd take a very public pledge, sober up for months running, and land a new job. He always did find that next job, because when he was sober he was good, and along the way he'd uncovered some big stories. But drink he did, and in his latest incarnation as a reporter for the *Metropolitan Meteor*, he was back at it, some said hard.

Martin loved the business though, and had been the only reporter on the paper to take the time to teach it to Gander, pointing out the little incongruities of the trade, initiating him into its tricks. For Martin Gale, being a reporter was a calling and, when Gander was still young and tense and new, Gale's stories about the old days were like a warm bath, his enthusiasm for his work a daily reminder to Gander that, in leaving the mail room, he had acquired much more than a new job. He'd found a profession. Gander's loyalty to Martin Gale was unconditional. Still, Gander had never been promoted beyond the Features Department. At thirty, with eight years of reporting under his belt, he still spent his days turning out features for Section B.

In Section B the Features Department had found a formula that was essentially a remedy for the day's news. In Section B it was not so much the facts that mattered; those you could get in the first section, or in the *Daily Mercury*. What counted was what you weaved around and through the facts, keeping it plausible but emotionally satisfying. Paul York, the Section B chief, and the other section editors saw it as their mission to soothe their readers' day-to-day anxieties. This was a philosophy summed up in the motto that figured prominently in the Section B masthead: Good News Never Hurt Anybody. Rather than dwell on the tired suffering that great cities have always bred, Section B overwhelmed its readers with kind, self-effacing people, content simply to smile out over italicized captions.

Martin Gale did little to disguise his distaste for Section B generally, and Paul York in particular, and Gander couldn't help but harbor his mentor's biases. But he had to be careful because Paul York was not an easy man to work for under the best of circumstances; he devoted far too much attention to his own ambitions to concern himself with the people working under him. And Gander's having asked to be promoted out of Features had only brought out York's worst side.

So Gander wrote his features, kept his job, and, still single, could live on his pay. He liked his apartment and could afford to take a girl out now and then. It took a little doing, but he stayed upbeat.

Ever since his parents' accident it had seemed important to look on the bright side, even if there were days when his paper's very name seemed merely a reminder of their crash through the guard-rail.

The *Meteor*: the night sky.

So he avoided referring to it as the *Meteor*, even though that's what everybody else in the city called it. He liked to think of it instead as the *Metropolitan*.

Gander stepped out of the elevator onto the twelfth floor of the *Metropolitan Meteor*, walked across the outer lobby, nodded at Harriet the receptionist, and started down a hall of framed front pages.

EXTRA! HE FLIES! EXTRA!
CAPED STRANGER SIGHTED:
MOTHER AND CHILD SAVED!

EXCLUSIVE! CAPED HERO
HAS A NAME: CALL ME
THE 'SUPERLATIVE MAN'

RADIO FLASH! SUPERLATIVE
MAN SPEAKS ON TRUTH
AND THE AMERICAN WAY

Turning down a hallway of office doors, and passing Paul York's empty office, he headed toward the last open door on the left where he shared a cubicle, one of six in the large room, with Buddy Lester, another features reporter. As he turned into the doorway, Patty Rose, the secretary, looked up from her desk. She sat just inside and answered phones and proofed type for the eleven sports and features writers sharing the space. Gander smiled at her, but she was rising from her chair, leaving her desk and coming toward him. As much as Gander would have liked to think that this pretty woman with hazel eyes and light waves of chestnut hair was drawn away from her work at the mere sight of him, he knew something was wrong.

"You haven't heard?" she asked, laying a hand on his arm.

He shook his head.

"It's Martin, Harvey. We just got a call. He had a heart attack and lost control of his car. The Superlative Man stopped it from going into a playground."

"Where?"

"Harvey, he's dead."

"*Where?*"

"Out by the old Foster School."

He turned on his heels, tore down the halls, past the framed front pages.

Foster School was less than a mile away, but the city had managed to plant a dozen red lights along the way. Gander lurched from one to the next, slamming his fist against the dashboard each time his car skidded to a stop, shouting at his windshield to make it change.

When he finally turned down Meadow Lane, he saw the ambulance parked in front of the school, a small crowd gathered behind it. Beyond them, children clustered at the playground's edge. Gander left his car in the middle of the street and pushed his way through. There on the pavement, stretched out flat on a low stretcher under the van's open door, lay Martin Gale, his necktie askew, his crumpled hat beside him on the roadway, his hands folded across his chest. He looked like he was sleeping.

Gander knelt beside him, wild with wonder at the freak mysteries of human existence. His parents' accident, and now Martin, a car careening out of control, the sudden appearance of the Superlative Man, children crowding in to see—it all blurred inside him, one picture collapsing into the next.

Someone behind him was speaking excitedly. He looked up. People standing around were looking skyward. He stopped crying.

The Superlative Man coursed across the gray sky, a receding point of scarlet and ivory, a tiny fluttering cape.

Something inside him moved. Faces all around him shone.

He backed his car down the street, turned around and headed in the direction of his office, rolling through one green light after another. Martin Gale had been no saint. But if it hadn't been for Martin, Gander might never have gotten out of that mail room. He had to mark this passing. He had to share this flashing red pain.

Back in his office he tapped out a heartfelt tribute to his mentor, concluding mighty lines and rolling cadences with the sudden appearance of the Superlative Man, the breathtaking diversion of Martin's car as it sped recklessly toward a crowded playground. The focus of the elegy metamorphosed from Martin, "an old-fashioned but big-hearted newsman," into this incredible phenomenon, this unhappy puzzle, this Superlative Man, who foresaw the speeding danger and raced from the sky to stand before the playground with an outstretched palm, who was able to save the children but unable to save Martin Gale. It all seemed inexplicably wrong, as though Martin had been tragically martyred simply to give the Superlative Man yet another chance to shine. The obituary grew into a lament for the human condition. We dangle like puppets, Gander wrote. We are the playthings of gods.

Powerful emotions gripped him as he wrote. He felt suddenly drawn into a common life with each and every person in the city, and at the same time sorrowfully aware of himself as a man alone. Some window deep inside him had opened.

But even as he typed the final words he sensed that, professionally, the piece could seal his fate in Features; for instead of showing himself capable of hard news, Gander had turned Martin's obituary, an almost-news story, into a vintage color piece. Without intending to, not really knowing what he intended when he sat down to write, he had produced a heartfelt tribute to a nobody, simply by arguing that, in death, no one is unimportant: all deserve to be saved. That his underlying motive might seem nothing less than a desire to take a swipe at the Superlative Man was beside the point. Those who read it could set it down reassured that it was still possible to die, an event usually reserved for News, and go on to Section B. And if they grew uneasy about Gander's unusually personal grievance against the Superlative Man, they might still sense that the article served another purpose. It somehow redeemed Martin from oblivion.

Ignoring his misgivings, Gander drew the last sheet from the roller, walked down the hall, and left the article on Paul York's chair.

The call came through an hour later.

"Gander? Paul York. You got a minute?"

"I'll be right there," Gander answered, second thoughts crowding in. Why had he done it? He should have waited before handing in the article. It was one thing to lose your head, but not about the Superlative Man, not in print.

He could see York through the glass wall, leaning forward in his chair, writing. He poked his head inside.

York looked up. "Gander. Come on in."

Gander waffled in the doorway. "Do you want me to close the door?"

"No, no. I'll be through in a second."

Gander sat straight back in a chair, waiting for York to finish, watching him. A shade past forty, York was a handsome man, though a little too manicured maybe. Someone once said his clothes were custom-tailored to fit the man he wished he was: some tycoon of understated elegance. However fine his clothes though, there was nothing understated about York's character. He was a domineering, self-serving man, with little compassion for anyone who didn't contribute to his lifelong campaign to enhance his own image. Which, of course, was just about everybody.

He had dressed in a dark-blue, chalk-striped suit and white shirt he looked born to wear, swirling blood-red detail in his tie, a gold braceleted watch at his wrist. Only his eyes let you past the immaculate, mannered surface: smoke-gray and haunted, they stared back like two ghastly drains. People worked hard for Paul York, courting the tailored phrases of his approval; but no one trusted him.

York lifted Gander's article from his desk and looked up. "This is an unusual piece," he began.

Gander caved in without resistance. "I shouldn't have handed it in. I'm sorry. I was upset."

York raised his eyebrows. A pause, and then: "No, Gander. It's okay. The piece is okay. I kind of like it." He laid it back on the desk.

"You do?"

"I do. It's from the heart. This guy meant something to you. We can print it. I'll add a little caption explaining that you worked together, so people will understand why it's got an edge. No, I like it. The piece is okay."

"This would mean a lot to me, York."

"I know, Gander. I know it would mean a lot to you."

York had a way of making himself hateful in the most unexpected ways. Gander waited for some signal that he was through, but York sat in his chair, leaning over his desk, rereading the obituary.

"Well, thanks," Gander suggested, starting from his chair.

"Wait a minute," York interrupted, and Gander sat back down. "There's something else. Did you know what Gale was working on when he died?"

"I haven't a clue."

York smiled vaguely.

"You know how it is," Gander explained quickly. "Martin was doing his stories down on ten and I've been up here chasing after features. We just didn't see each other every day."

"You two didn't keep up? I thought he sort of looked out for you."

"He did, in his way. I owed him a lot. But he never talked much about the stories he was on until he thought they were ready to print."

"A few days ago he did a piece. People overdosing down in the Southern Tier. You saw it?"

"I saw it, sure, but I didn't know it was Martin's. There wasn't any byline."

"That's true. But it was."

"It was just a squib, really."

"That's true, too," York allowed, "but Gale told me he thought there was more to it. What do you think? You want to follow it up?"

"*News?*"

"Sure, why not. It's a little out of the ordinary, but the boys down on ten don't need to know. We'll keep it between us. Take a shot and see where it goes."

"Paul York, I've waited for this."

"So I gathered."

"If there's anything in it, I swear I'll get it for you."

"Good." York pulled open his top right drawer, drew out a single piece of paper, and set it before him on top of Martin Gale's obituary. "I want you to go back and double-check that article we ran, Monday I think it was. Then you can start with this list of names. Martin gave it to me. He said these are the known ODs." York slid the list across the desk. "See what you can find."

"Sure," Gander agreed. "When do you want it?"

York reached around to a small table behind him. He turned back with a thick file folder in his hand. "Tomorrow night's fine," he answered, opening the file and beginning to read.

"Tomorrow night," Gander repeated.

York looked up. "No good?"

"No, no, it's fine."

Gander waited for him to say something more, but York was reading. The interview was over.

Patty looked up as Gander hurried into the office.

"Patty," he whispered, leaning over her desk, a single finger to his lips.

"What?" she whispered back.

"Not a word. I just got a news assignment."

"Harvey, that's terrific!" she said.

"Shh!"

"Sorry," she whispered back.

"It was Martin's."

"And York gave it to *you?*"

Gander straightened up. "Sure. Why not?"

"Since when is York handing out news assignments?"

"Search me. But I've got it, and it was Martin's."

Patty shifted. "I'm going to miss him."

Gander said, "So am I," and their eyes met. "How well did you know him?"

"Not very. But he always seemed like such a sweet guy."

"Patty, maybe you could help me."

"Oh?"

"I know you're busy, but York gave me a list of people over-dosing down in the Southern Tier. You could do an index check on their names, see if anything turns up. Not too far back. Maybe six months? A year if you have the time?"

"I could do that," she agreed, "but it'll have to wait until to-morrow. It's almost six-thirty as it is."

"Maybe by noon?"

"I'll try. How many are there?"

Gander looked down at the piece of paper in his hand, scanning the names for the first time. Five names in Martin's wobbly hand.

"Albert Long," he said.

"Pardon?"

"Albert Long is on this list."

"And?"

"If it's the same guy, I knew him, or at least I knew who he was."

"And?"

"No, nothing. I didn't know him real well, but he used to hang out down at High Water."

"The bar?"

"Yeah. I'd go down there and see him sometimes."

"What about the others?"

"No, I don't think so," Gander answered, rereading the list. He looked up. "There are only five names here," he answered her.

"One down, four to go."

"Maybe. But check on Albert Long, just in case." He smiled awkwardly. "What a coincidence. I haven't been to High Water in ages."

High Water

It was almost nine when he finally left his office and started uptown, walking back along Seventh Avenue, past his apartment, past the gates into Carnival Park and on down Carnival Street. And he just kept going, kept thinking about Martin Gale and his new assignment, thinking about High Water.

At the corner of Fifth and Tenth he waited for a light by a bronze statue of a cash register, something the city had commissioned expecting the artist to create a tribute to the Nation's Financial Capital. The corner was promptly dubbed "Five and Dime." He walked to Soldiers' Road and sat in a small memorial plaza on the median strip, on a great stone bench under a sunfaced clock. Half an hour later he entered the north end of the park, passed an occasional family curled up on blankets under the wide awning of a tree, trying to beat apartment heat. He lapped once around the reservoir, appearing like the stroke of a pendulum in the dirty gold of periodic lamps that stood sentry around the water, the black water beside him illumining in sudden ruffled patches.

Swing into light. Swing to black. Head back down Reservoir Road and stand in the sudden rain.

The night teemed dull silver. He glanced at his watch, the face blearing. A quarter past ten.

Flipping up his lapels, he went to the curb edge to get a better look at the street signs. Looking up was hopeless. The names ran like dreams when you wake. But it looked like Buffalo and Forge, and Buffalo and Forge sounded right. He turned on his soles and ran two and a half blocks to a narrow side street, ran halfway down Stage Alley and stood under a black canvas overhang, the entrance to High Water. Above the overhang a blinking sign marked red time, the slow neon freezing a thousand falling faces in the rain.

He knew this place. But it had been a while.

High Water was an old hangout for newspaper types. But there were a few legitimate theaters in the neighborhood and it served a transient crowd. Actors and actresses haunted it. Yet although the nightclub sat in the rear basement of a theater, most people in the audience on a given night had never even heard of it. Stage Alley ran behind the Barnhouse Theater, which had been built into a blocklong slope and had a front entrance two flights higher than the pavement of Stage Alley. Whoever designed it had dug about four stories down into the hillside, making space for storage or changing or practicing, clearing out the land straight back to Stage Alley, so that even on the Stage Alley side there was a deep basement. There were more rooms under the Barnhouse than in a lot of small office buildings, and for a long time most of them sat empty, or collected old costumes, or dust. Then an ex-newsman named Max Water took a long lease on a handful of them, painted a sign saying Come Hell or High Water, and hung his name on the door.

Gander used to stop by as a young reporter, figuring it was something you did if you were in the business, and while there he'd listen to newsmen broadcast secrets about whoever was hot on the next day's front page. It was a way of keeping up on things, a chance to get closer to real news.

And besides, there were the actresses. Late one night he met one and took to sneaking out of her rooming house at four-thirty in the morning. Then one day she said, I'm sorry, Harvey, and it was over.

You could get tired of High Water.

He hadn't been by in over a year, but he had run into Frankie Bullock in an uptown diner just a few weeks ago. Frankie had posted himself on a stool in High Water every night since the place opened. And he knew all about Gander's actress, he said, or at least he'd heard all about her. He'd heard about her agent, too, and the story was that her agent told her to get smart: if she was going to sleep around, she should stick to guys who could return the favor and put her on a stage now and then. She told him to get lost, but later that week got a bit part in some hot new director's hot new play.

Gander, explained Frankie, the man of many ears, you were history.

And Gander listened silently, thinking: Nice talking to you, Frankie, you bastard.

"Good to see you, Gander. Eat here often?"

Not anymore.

You can't argue with a guy like Frankie Bullock. He'd listen to whatever you had to say, wander down to his perch at High Water, and tell anyone who happened to be sitting next to him what a sorry chump that Gander was. As though he, the Bullock himself, had only been trying to help, but one man could do just so much. But Gander had been tempted, if not to argue then to hit him in the face with a plate of mashed potatoes and gravy.

Frankie's monologue had started the wheels turning again. If so much time hadn't slipped by, Gander might have gone looking for her that night. Not that he had anything to say, unless it was to tell her that sleeping around wasn't exactly the way he'd describe making love with her every night for three months. But if she didn't know it, she didn't know it. And it was too late to go looking for her to tell her she didn't know it. Even if she'd only walked out on him yesterday, it would have been too late for that.

So it was by association that High Water seemed a closed chapter. First she turns around and walks out of his life, then his parents plunge off a cliff. It had been easier to quit the place than to stand around explaining how he felt about all this. Why was she on one side of the room and he another? And what did he think about the Superlative Man after what had happened? People do ask these things, especially of a guy like Gander, whom they think they have pegged until a girl like Violet Hayes comes along and slides her arm through his. They were interested in that, no question. Enter Violet and suddenly the world sees a future in Section B. Exit Violet and you could get tired of High Water. You could get tired of standing around drinking by yourself, listening to other men gossip about your profession, or your personal life if you interrupted. It was better to go home. Drink there.

But here he was back at High Water tonight. And he was kidding himself if he pretended he was thinking only about his new assignment.

Gander opened the front door and descended a short flight of concrete steps to a swinging door. He pushed through and stood inside.

Polka-dotted with green and white lights, the room was awash in pale aqua. A dark bar lined the left wall opposite a wall lined with booths, each with a small shaded lamp. Scattered across the black-and-white tiled floor in between were round tables and wooden picket-backed chairs. At the far end of the room, on a slight stage in a cloud of rose light, a piano man seemed absorbed in the movement of his hands.

Half the tables, chairs, and booths went empty, but men's backs packed the bar. A lone empty stool spelled a narrow space halfway down. Two bartenders hustled back and forth. Gander waited to make eye contact with the one he recognized.

"Gander. Where ya been?" he said, already passing, looking over his shoulder, a wet glass in each hand.

"Not here," Gander answered on the return trip, clusters of empties on the bartender's fingers.

The bartender slowed on the third pass. "So I noticed. Everything okay?"

"Just great."

"What brings you by?"

"Couldn't be the alcohol."

"Not a chance."

"Or the rain."

"Yeah? It's raining? You know, in here I never know," he said, looking toward the door. He looked back at Gander and added matter-of-factly, "You're wet."

"It was something I had to know, Steve. I'm only glad it was you."

Steve laughed somewhere behind his teeth. His eyes never left Gander's. "What'll it be? Scotch and water?"

"I'm impressed."

"Never forget a drink."

"A glass of beer."

"You got it."

A moment later a tall wet glass of beer stood on the bar and Steve was stalking his line of patrons, trading glasses back and forth across the flat wood. Gander lifted his glass, carried it across the room to an empty booth, and slid in on a bench facing the door.

. . .

The glass sat empty on the table, Gander wondering if he even knew anyone still coming around, when someone behind him spoke.

"Long time no see."

He recognized the voice before he saw the face. The piano man appeared beside him, leaning forward with an outstretched hand.

Gander took it. "Billy," he said.

"I saw you come in. You been a stranger."

"So I hear. Sit down."

"Just for a couple minutes. I gotta play some life into this joint."

"What's going on? It's so quiet."

"It'll pick up."

"It's just I don't see any of the old faces."

"Everything around here's new. Water sold out. New people running things. Surprised you didn't hear. Kept the same faces out front. That's about all."

"I saw Steve."

"Steve, me, some others. Our paycheck says Semblance of Continuity."

"I guess it has been a while."

"New crowd, Gander, whole new crowd. You'll see if you stick around." And then his voice faded to a whisper: "Violet still comes around. You don't want to see her, Gander."

Gander could barely make out the words Billy's voice was so low. He answered, "You're looking good, Billy."

"Me? I'm the same. You look different, though."

"I'll get over it. It's been a long day."

Billy Bolder said, "Don't bother. It suits you," and laughed, his head back, a gold tooth shining in the low light. "I'm headin' back to work. See you around?"

"Why not. Get them dancing," Gander said, nodding at the backs of the men at the bar.

He nursed a second beer, the place filling up. People drank and talked at the tables and in the booths. A couple danced below Billy in his rose light, on his low stage. But still Gander saw no one he knew, no one he could approach, no one he could start a casual conversation with, then steer it around to Albert Long. And he was still sitting there, watching the door, when he heard her voice over his shoulder, saying his name.

He looked back uncertain—as though he weren't dead sure who'd spoken. "Well, hello yourself," he answered.

Violet Hayes.

"What a surprise," she said, eyes glistening.

"It's me," he admitted. "In the flesh."

"You can keep your clothes on," she teased.

"I wouldn't want to get cold standing in line," he answered and immediately regretted it.

Colors in her face moved. She looked like she was going to hit him or cry. She did neither. "I only wanted to say hi. I'm sorry."

What she was sorry about she didn't say. She just stood there, not leaving, not sitting down. Thinner than he'd ever seen her. Pale Violet in a green dress. In a green dress cupping her small high white breasts and curling sideways at her stockinged calves, with hair the color of bright sand, even in the aqua light. And long black eyelashes and wide dark eyes. Almost too wide, as if looking out from some pitch-black place, too dark in her white face. Her bare shoulders leaned in as though the room behind her were cold, the neckline of her dress plunging between her breasts, showing off their inner white curves, her nipples protruding underneath the thin cloth. The thin green cloth that clung to her waist, caved at her sex, creased between her thighs.

A small gold chain braceleted her ankle. She watched him watching her, watched him taking in her body. She was the same and she wasn't. Paler, thinner, scared.

Her expression changed rapidly, touching anger, touching annoyance. She brushed back a flock of hair with her fingers.

"Miss me?" she said.

He didn't answer.

Two fingers lingered in her hair at her cheek. "I'm not so bad," she ventured.

"Wear it on a sign," he said. "You stop by to tell me that?"

"I thought maybe you came to see me."

"You're kidding. You're kidding me."

Her hand waved in front of her face. "I just needed to sit *down* for a second, okay? I'll go away."

Gander gestured loosely at the opposite bench and she wavered but slid onto it, leaning back flat against the green seat.

"How's tricks?" he said. He couldn't help it.

"Stop it!" Violet hissed. "I said I was *sorry*. You want me to say it again? I'm sorry, I'm sorry! Can I just sit down? Can I just sit down, please?"

Her whole body trembled. She looked like she was freezing to death.

"Violet, I'm . . . Just forget it."

"I forget everything. What else? Give me something else."

"Are you all right?"

"Terrific."

"What've you been doing?"

"None of your business."

"I can't believe it," he said.

"I didn't mean it that way. Let's not talk about me. What about you?"

"Me? Oh, I'm great. Take today. Just great."

"I only wanted to say hi." She slid to the edge of the seat, starting away. "I didn't think I needed a reason."

"Violet."

She stopped.

"Stay here with me."

"Harvey," she said, her hand reaching across the table. "I just needed somebody to talk to."

"So talk to me. Stay here and talk to me."

Violet stirred a plastic stick in her whiskey ice. She looked up at Gander and pressed her lips into a flat smile. A tiny vein throbbed in her neck, another on her temple above her ear. Her eyes shone. They were someplace else.

He never had known how old she was. Twenty-four, maybe, with most of the last years spent trying to get onstage. No shortage of auditions, though. Her agent always raised eyebrows just parading her down runways. But she lived on walk-ons. In three years she'd had two speaking parts. Until one day she got her chance. Gander saw the reviews and wished he hadn't. She had half a dozen lines in the first act and the last. A cast of eight, and three critics zeroed in on her: a mannequin with strings. A beautiful statue, but you wished she didn't bother coming to life.

Now the veins pulsed in her head. She looked like she felt like hell.

"You look pretty," Gander said. He felt bad about what he'd said.

"You mean it?" The plastic stick stopped stirring.

"I mean it. You look good."

"Liar. Thanks anyway."

"You working?"

"What?" She hadn't heard him.

"Acting, you do it for a living."

Her face was still. Her eyes blurred. It wasn't crying. "Let's just say I took up modeling."

"You'd be a good model."

"That's all I ever hear. It means forget acting. People get tired of feeling sorry for you.

"Harvey." Her voice was so faint he could barely hear it. "Let's switch tracks, okay?"

"I hear Water sold out," he said.

She nodded, chewing the plastic stick, looking along the backs of the men lining the bar. She looked suddenly at Gander. "What did you say?"

"Water sold out."

"Oh. Yeah, he sold."

"How come?"

She watched him a moment. "What difference does it make?"

"You like modeling?"

"Some investors," she answered.

"You don't have to sit here. I don't mind. But nobody's making you or anything."

Her eyes brightened. "You're not trying to make me?"

Seasonal Violet. Her moods changed, like weather. Everything looked a little brighter, and she smiled, not at Gander, but to herself.

"Maybe you're trying to make me," he suggested.

"Mind if I taste your beer?" she asked.

He slid it across the polished wooden surface, leaving a wake of condensation. "Help yourself."

She looked into the glass, her lips moving. "Harvey, can I talk to you about something?"

"Whatever you got."

"Sometimes I get scared."

"About what?"

"I don't know. It's hard to explain. Things really changed."

"I know. I hardly recognize a soul."

"It's not just that. Water sold the place, it's true. But it's these new men running things."

"What about them?"

Her voice faded and she leaned forward, practically mouthing the words: "People are getting killed down here."

Gander leaned forward and met her half way. "Who?" he said.

"Just people you see. The papers finally picked it up, last week I think, and I was waiting for more, but so far there hasn't been anything."

"Albert Long was one of them?"

"Yeah. How did you know?"

"The paper said it was an overdose."

"I know, but it's not true. They killed him."

"Why?"

"He was the same as the rest. They all got rescued by the Superlative Man."

"They're getting killed because they were rescued by the Superlative Man?"

"Shut *up*, Harvey," Violet whispered furiously. "Are you trying to get *me* killed?"

"Violet, I'm sorry, I'm sorry. No one heard, okay?"

"I'm just edgy, *okay*?"

"But it's true?"

"I told you."

"Why?"

"They killed Albert Long because one night he got drunk right here at the bar and Steve cut him off. He started yelling about how nobody could do that to him. Then he just lost it. I mean, he could barely stand up, but he was screaming at Steve that nobody could touch him because he knew where the Harem was."

"The what?"

"Forget it. It's just a place."

"A bar?"

"No, not really." And again her voice faded, Gander reading her lips to make out the words: "It's an old casket factory down by the river. Albert Long *was* an overdose. But they did it to him."

"Violet, what are you talking about? What are you *doing* here?"

She leaned back, pinning her shoulders against the green cushion. "It's just so hard to leave. I mean it, Harvey. Sometimes I get scared."

A woman screeched. *"Violet! Darling!"* Violet looked paralyzed. A woman in the next booth kneeled on her seat, looking down over the high-backed divider at Harvey and Violet. "You *did* come! *After* all!" The enthusiastic intruder had one pitch. All exclamation. No song.

Violet turned like a block of wood. "Jeannie. You startled me."

Jeannie appeared around the divider in a flashy red dress with lots of bosom, a pound or so of icy jewelry, and black hair piled atop her head. But it was her face that gave her away. Jeannie was in ecstasy.

"Violet, my *darling* girl." Her voice dropped abruptly. "Did you say you were scared, honey?"

"Don't be silly, Jeannie. I said startled. You startled both of us."

"And here I could have sworn you said you were scared." Her voice rising again. "But don't I get intro*duced*?"

"Harvey Gander," said Harvey Gander.

"Harvey Gander," she repeated. "I've heard your name. Nice. Real nice. You call me Jeannie." She squeezed her eyes and her voice turned confidential. "Here I've been sitting here and sitting here, waiting for Violet to come through that door. And what do I hear?"

She paused. Gander watched her.

"Violet! In the next booth! When *did* you get here?"

"A little while ago," Violet answered.

The two women stared at one another. "I was getting worried," Jeannie said.

"You shouldn't have," said Violet.

"But now I've found you and I'm not letting go."

"Jeannie," Violet said. "I'm sorry."

Jeannie's smile grew. "Don't I get to sit down?" she asked.

"Sit down," Gander suggested.

"You're sweet. Thanks. But now I've gone and butted in. You have to let me buy the next round."

She glided away and was gone, gesturing to the bartender, the one Gander didn't know, as she crossed the room toward the bar.

"Forget it," Violet whispered, "just forget everything."

At the end of the bar, the bartender leaned his head down and Jeannie spoke into his ear, touching his shoulder and gesturing with her other hand toward Harvey and Violet, the bartender looking directly at them. Jeannie started back across the room on her red high heels, Harvey smiling broadly at her.

"Now don't ask what I ordered," she warned, sliding onto the bench. "It's my house special and it's on me."

"Your house?"

"Nice, isn't it? Though it's not *really* mine. I share it with friends. They bought it from Mr. Water himself."

"What for?"

"Why, free drinks!"

"Well, why not."

Jeannie blew him a kiss, her hand palm out at her chin. Gander feigned a hit to his cheek and Jeannie smiled approvingly. Violet sat upright beside her, arching her back and stretching, her fists at her shoulders.

"Atta girl, Violet," Jeannie encouraged. "Don't look so glum."

Violet's hands fell into her lap. "You're sweet. I *need* one of those drinks."

The bartender arrived with a tray, set the drinks on the table, and left without a word. Jeannie did the honors, passing them around.

"Sure, honey, sure," she replied, handing out the drinks. "Drink up and everybody gets a prize. I get a parasol and Violet gets a thingamajig and Harvey gets a special. Can I call you Harvey?"

Gander held up a red spear in the pressed shape of a naked woman. "This drink is green," he said.

"It's my special."

"It's green."

She looked at him reprovingly. "For me?"

It tasted like medicine.

Billy Bolder started to play.

Or he had been playing and it only seemed like he'd started.

Remote voices drifted in across a speaker system.

Everyone was turning up the volume.

"End of the play," Violet called out.

"I don't think he understands," Jeannie answered.

"I'm listening, I'm listening," Gander assured them, wondering if his drink had been drugged. "I'm listening," he loudly repeated.

"You're listening?" Jeannie coaxed.

Gander nodded vigorously.

Violet's mouth was moving. She was also talking too loud. "Hey, Jeannie," she exclaimed, her eyes glowing, "let's have *fun*!" Violet's drink was drugged, too.

"Anything you say, sweetheart."

The conversation on the loudspeakers kept getting louder. Then the room got quieter and it was just the loudspeakers, but when Gander looked around him people still seemed to be talking. Billy stopped playing.

"What's that *talking*," Gander said.

"Let's dance," Violet announced. "Harvey. Wanna dance?"

"What's that on the *speakers*?"

Jeannie pointed at the roof. "Upstairs. End of the play," she explained, mouthing the words.

Violet screeched, "Harvey!" as though remembering something important.

"What *is* it?"

She looked over at him and burst out laughing. "Wanna *dance*?"

"What's in these drinks?"

"Don't be silly," Jeannie said.

Nobody was allowed to be silly at High Water.

"Harvey," Violet cautioned, "you be nice to Jeannie. Ask her if you can come along tonight."

"Can I come along tonight?"

"Violet, honey, you're high."

"High. Bye." Violet smiled like a cat and Gander undressed her with his eyes. Her face glowed.

"This drink is green," he said.

"Come with *us*, Harvey. Jeannie calls it Candy Land."

"Violet!" Jeannie reprimanded, but smiled at Gander. "Your friend may have other plans."

"Not me," Gander dismissed the notion, waving a hand in front of his face.

"Neither do we," Jeannie concluded, still smiling. "But maybe some other time. We'll see." Gander was tired of watching her smile. He wanted to watch her go away. He changed his mind. He wanted to dance with Violet. Let's dance, Violet. Violet poked her finger into her drink, into her mouth, into her drink. She held it out to Gander. Oh, Jeannie, go away.

"Sorry you have to leave so soon," Jeannie regretted.

"Not me," he assured her.

"Oh, but you do," she assured him.

"Violet," Gander said, ignoring Jeannie, "let's go."

"Make me," Violet said and burst out laughing.

.   .   .

He stood alone in the middle of the floor. Violet was gone. Jeannie sat across the room in the booth. He turned and the room broke into applause.

Rain inside a box.

A line of faces. Men line the bar. They look over their shoulders. They pound the bar and hoot like geese.

Violet standing at the end of the bar, her face in profile.

Violet.

And the empty piano stage.

Everything drowning in applause.

And neon rain.

Standing in the red neon rain.

Natasha Nyle

He slid his arms into the sleeves of his dressing gown, his worn black slippers flopping across the carpet as he tied the cloth belt loosely at his waist. He descended to the vestibule, picked up the morning paper, and was reading the lead story on the front page as he climbed back up the stairs.

He never saw her coming. Never heard her high heels.

She was just there, her breasts approaching beyond the top edge of his newspaper, shaping the snow-clean cloth of a summer dress. Gander let the newspaper fall to his side, but she was already descending past him, and he turned and watched the fall of blond hair under her wide hat, the white cotton dress, her tapering back, the full curve of her rump, the lilt of white linen, falling, a step at a time. Until the first-floor landing, where she stopped, her white-ribboned, wide straw hat turning slightly, still concealing her face as she turned to walk back up the stairs, the hat brim angled so that he could not see her face, even as she brushed past, even as her hand slipped into his, drawing him up the stairs. And he followed, a swimmer swallowed in the undertow, his face at her back, looking up into the sunny waves of her hair. She led him through the open door of his apartment but loosed his hand, keeping her back to him, pressing her body gently against the inside of the door, pressing it closed, then stepping back, careful to keep her hat brim between them, careful not to face him, her hands moving unseen down the front of her dress, her arms stretching up and over her head and the dress falling away to the floor, a cascade of snow-white cloth rising at her feet like foam. Naked, her back to him, a pitcher of cream. Drink me. And only then he understood. Only then he said, No. And the answer, Yes, her voice falling, Yes, as she stepped out of her high heels, as she turned, her hat rising. As she smiled. Violet Hayes.

Gander stared down over his paper at the woman in the white dress standing in his lobby and looking inquisitively back, her hand on the knob to the front door of his apartment building. He watched her as she turned, as she walked through the doorway, the door closing behind her, the bright opaque panes of glass, the single clear pane looking out across the stoop into the sun-washed street. In the perfect quiet, in the shadowed hall, he climbed the sagging hardwood stairs, the morning paper at his side. "I'm hallucinating," he muttered quietly, the taste of the green drink haunting his brain.

He held the kitchen phone against his cheek, listening to it ring.

"Hello?" she answered.

"Patty, it's me. Harvey."

"You sound *awful*."

"I just woke up."

"Do you know what time it is?"

Gander glanced at his empty wrist. "No," he said.

"It's almost one."

Gander rolled his eyes.

"Harvey?"

"I'm here."

"Wait till you hear. All those overdoses? Every one of them was saved last spring by the Superlative Man."

"I know."

"What do you mean, you know?"

"I heard it last night."

"What else did you hear? I just spent half the morning on this."

"I'm sorry, Patty, I . . ."

"I know, you just woke up."

"But I'm going to need you to do something else."

"Why not?" she said.

"I need some names of people who were rescued who aren't dead."

"Pardon?"

"I've got no place to start. All I have is a list of people rescued by the Superlative Man and they're all dead. I need some who aren't dead yet."

"Just anybody?"

"No. What about Albert Long? Did you find anything on him?"

Patty said, "You know those double rescues that started last spring?"

"Sure," Gander answered slowly.

"Albert Long was one of them. I had the article out about half an hour ago."

"So that's where we start."

"All right. Hold on a second."

Gander waited, looking across his kitchen into the sunshine.

"I've got one," Patty announced.

"One what?"

"The name of the other person rescued when Albert Long was saved. I told you, I just had it out a little while ago. Her name's Natasha Nyle and she lives in the Outer Borough. There's a picture of her with the Superlative Man. She's gorgeous, Harvey. And listen to this story." Gander leaned against the kitchen wall, his ear to the phone.

An hour later he stood across the street from Natasha Nyle's brownstone, on a sidewalk in the Outer Borough.

The number on the row house matched the seven on the piece of paper in his hand. Three rows of three windows shone, a square of nine, each window a golden mirror in the afternoon sun, except for the middle window in the top row, the only open one: half golden glass, half shadow, a hand draped over the sill.

From a distance Gander couldn't be certain. It looked like a woman's hand, and three was the apartment number she had given him over the phone. The third floor. But the hand became a thin forearm, then seemed simply to stop, perhaps continuing on in a dark sleeve, invisible in the shadow, perhaps disappearing behind a curtain. Whatever it was, the effect unsettled him, and he called out absurdly: "Miss Nyle! Miss Nyle!," as though faced with some minor emergency that left no time for the politics of walking up to the front door, ringing the bell, and announcing himself over the intercom. *"Miss Nyle!"* His voice floating out over the quiet side street, two blocks from a humming boulevard. In the answering silence the hand withdrew.

He stared at the pavement as he walked, crossing the street to climb the few steps of the stone stoop and stopping at the top to reread yet again the piece of paper in his hand. When it exploded at his feet.

A large, shriveled gourd lay obscenely on the landing. Gander peered up the face of the building to the sky. No one. The single half-open window at the top sat empty.

Maybe it was an accident. You just happened to be standing there. Maybe it was a coincidence.

The woman had sounded agreeable enough on the phone, Gander recalled. Heavily accented, some foreign perfume, but accommodating. Agreeable. ("I would be happy to share my story with you. But I can't guess why anyone would want to read it." And the usual assurances: "Why, certainly they'll read it. Certainly they'll read about you.")

Somewhere overhead a woman laughed, the sound sourceless and circling over the street like a small talking wind. Gander stepped over the gourd into the vestibule, glancing back to the street, wondering who else had seen it fall.

He pressed the black button beside the name Natasha Nyle. Immediately the small square intercom spat a frazzled static. But no one greeted him. He waited, listening, and at last ventured, "Miss Nyle?"

And a waiting voice answered, "Yes?" then paused again before saying: "Mr. Gander?"

"Harvey Gander. *Metropolitan Meteor.*"

"You may come up."

A tortured buzzer rang, and Gander took the stairs two at a time to the third floor, but stopped abruptly on the final landing before a single unmarked door, slightly ajar, a forgotten key in the lock. He wondered whether or not to remove it. He had it between his fingers, when Natasha Nyle called out from somewhere inside.

"Come in, come in," she sang, then added, "I will be with you."

Gander pushed at the door. It swung slowly into an empty living room, sunlight pouring through the half-open window at the far end.

"Miss Nyle?" he called.

He stepped in, closing the door behind him.

"Miss Nyle?" he repeated to the empty room. Modest and unremarkable, the living area was long but sparsely furnished, boasting little more than a brown sofa, two cream-colored chairs, and a low coffee table bare of magazines and books, bare of anything but a tiny stone figure centered in the oval surface.

Two tall bookcases behind the sofa attracted his attention. Lined with knickknacks and bric-a-brac, even from a distance they conjured a picture of the woman who must have collected and arranged them so precisely, and he wandered to the sofa and leaned over it, his hands resting on the sofa back. A tiny animal horn lay centered in a landscape of scraps and souvenirs, tiny figurines and miniature pictures, a purple intaglio, a single yellow earring, a Tarot card facedown, a green liqueur glass with a golden rim, a fat-bellied stone dog, and, above it all, on a shelf alone, a photograph of a beautiful young woman in a tuxedo: she had long wavy black hair and sported a conical party hat, long streamers at the peak pouring down. Her face blended with the picture of Natasha Nyle forming in Gander's mind: a foreign woman in a party hat, with long black hair and a single pale hand, laughing.

Gander stood over the coffee table, looking down at the solitary stone figure on the flat wooden surface. He picked it up to examine it. It was a small stone man, with barely defined fingers and toes and an absurdly oversize face, with ears like tiny handles and no mouth whatsoever, not even a line of pursed lips above the steeply receding chin, but with wide-set, glittering red stones for eyes. It looked like the head of an insect.

"Mr. Gander."

He pivoted.

"I startled you," she continued. "I'm sorry." The foreign inflections. Natasha Nyle.

He had been so absorbed in the face of the little bug-eyed, jug-eared man, he had forgotten he wasn't alone. But he now stared at a woman with the face of the woman in the photograph. She had the same long black hair, and she wore a long, low-cut black dress hugging tight to the curves of her body and black high heels.

But she had the bulging red eyes of the little stone man.

She spoke: "Is everything all right? Mr. Gander?"

And then the laughter, high, light, disembodied; the black sheath of her body seeming not to move, her lips open slightly, her red eyes shining, the laughter coming from somewhere inside her.

The green drink.

"I'm hallucinating again," Gander said softly, perching on the edge of the sofa and automatically replacing the little stone man at the center of the coffee table. "I'm hallucinating," he repeated to himself.

She said, "Perish the thought."

He looked up from the table.

"It's lively in here today," she added.

What did she say? he wondered, her lips no longer moving, his mind roaming through static. The red was fading from her eyes, leaving them wide and black. Her face was deathly white, narrow and high-boned, with flesh so pale it blurred at the surface. Her lips were painted bright red. Long black hair poured down across her left shoulder, across her pale white chest, her dress a long stroke of black to the carpet. In the middle of the day. A woman clothed in her own silhouette. Gander's eyes lifted to hers. Large, bright, and black, they shone in recognition.

"You're so absorbed!" she said.

"I was," he admitted, then smiled purposefully, all he could manage.

"Ah, and now you're back."

Like intricate needlework highlighting plain cloth, her accent interlaced her words. Each word in and of itself was clear and familiar, but the flow of foreign inflections advanced in halting, lilting sequences.

And then, without apparent provocation, she laughed, light and high. "You had the expression on your face when you turned!" she exclaimed.

51

"Which expression?"

"A manner of speaking. Sit."

He sank back against the sofa, and she glided sideways across the carpet to one of the cream-colored chairs, twisting rather than bending her body to the chair's contour, turning in a sort of double helix until her black high heels and white face seemed poised to float in opposite directions.

"It is curious of you to think of me," she offered, "to want to talk to me." Her face drifted toward the sunlight. "What happened is now, oh, several months ago?"

"I saw your picture," Gander lied.

"On the shelf?" she suggested, her hand fluttering away to the bookcase behind him.

"The picture of you with the Superlative Man. In the paper."

"Oh?"

"You didn't see it?" he asked.

"I didn't say that, Mr. Gander," she answered, but stared at him a fraction of a second too long. She was thinking, perhaps deciding how to respond. And then, as if to preclude his pursuing it further, she stood and approached across the carpet, stopping only when she was so close to his face he could have leaned forward and reached his arms around her hips. He looked up her torso, her face hovering above the two rolling curves of her breasts, long black hair tapering down. She bent over at her waist, her face floating before him, her breasts quavering behind the hanging neckline of her dress.

"Would you mind very much," she asked, "if I sat beside you? It is so much less awkward than speaking across the room."

She slipped to the cushion beside him, her arm snaking along the top of the sofa behind him, and for the first time since entering the apartment, Gander thought of the gourd landing on the stoop.

The question popped out: "You didn't by any chance drop a gourd out your window, did you?"

"A what?" she sang, sitting up and slightly away, in mock recoil.

"A gourd . . . I mean . . . Sorry," he concluded, and then mumbled: "A kid on the roof."

"No. You must tell me. A gourd!"

"Nothing, it was nothing." She refused to take her eyes off him. "A gourd." He fumbled. "It fell on the steps."

"How intriguing," she murmured. Her dark eyes gleamed in her white face.

"Listen, Miss Nyle," he blurted.

"Natasha, please."

"Natasha. I'm doing a story. It's a series, actually. About people saved by the Superlative Man."

"But surely this has been done before," she suggested, her hands curled in her lap, her back arched, her eyes glancing sideways at him from under her brows.

"Well that's true. But people read this sort of thing."

She eyed him. "Oh?"

Only at that moment did Gander realize he had no idea how to explain what he wanted from her. He couldn't simply announce that he'd stumbled onto a connection between the overdoses and the rescues. Could he? Wasn't it too soon for that? But then, what was he doing here? What would she think?

He plunged ahead.

"A while back the Superlative Man saved a whole slew of people. You too. He saved some others but I'm just looking at certain people."

"This is so interesting," she said, leaning her shoulder into his, concentrating her attention on him, trying to purse her lips but managing merely to plump them, as though waiting to be kissed.

"Well, it is interesting," Gander answered, drawing his shoulder slightly away and turning on the seat cushion to face her. "You see, I was assigned to do a story about these people, but it seems they have only two things in common. The first is that they were all rescued by the Superlative Man."

"I see," she answered, turning in place, as he had, to face him, one leg curled beneath her, her knee touching his. The fingertips of her hand alighted on his chest. "And I am one of these people?"

He concentrated on her eyes. "No, the people I'm writing about are all dead, which is the other thing they have in common. They all died of drug overdoses. Which is why you're interesting."

"Because I'm not dead?"

Gander nodded encouragingly. "And you were saved under pretty extraordinary circumstances. Which isn't so unusual. This is the Superlative Man, after all. But just when you were in danger and could have been killed, just at that moment the Superlative Man was way over on the other side of the city and face-to-face with a dilemma."

"Really," she offered without emphasis, sliding down on her elbow against the cushions, her face resting on her hand.

"There you were," Gander elaborated, "hanging from some awning high over the street. And the Superlative Man needed to save you *and* race off to stop that runaway train. It was a close call. Remember? That train was heading into the city."

She nodded, rolling onto her back, stretching her legs, her eyes staring down her belly to the low coffee table.

"The conductor was drugged," Gander explained. "But the Superlative Man got there in the nick of time. There've been close calls like that, one right after the other. Everybody's been writing about it. The Superlative Man's greatest season."

She closed her eyes, and Gander asked, "Natasha?" just to be sure.

"I am listening," she answered. "Please continue."

"Of course, the Superlative Man can't save everybody," Gander observed. "Look around. People die every day. But now it seems even getting saved by the Superlative Man isn't enough, since later on you could end up as just another drug overdose."

"Mr. Gander," she interrupted, opening her eyes and sitting up to face him. "You were leading up to something?" Her back straight, her hands folded primly in her lap.

"Well, doesn't it strike you as sort of odd?" Gander asked.

"That some people take drugs?" she asked.

"That certain people rescued by the Superlative Man end up overdosing."

"You mean coincidences," she suggested.

"Coincidences? You think?"

"What do *you* think?" she chided him and tossed a hand in the air. "This is some suicide conspiracy?"

"I don't think I said exactly that, Natasha. But I was starting to wonder. What if these people all knew each other?"

"Would that be so strange?"

"Sure, because it'd be too *much* of a coincidence. You see, what I don't get is why they're all being killed."

"*Killed!*"

"No, listen," Gander answered, swept away with the idea. "Think about it. What if they knew too much? What if there was something funny about the rescues? Natasha, think about your own rescue. Who else was there when you fell off the balcony? Was anyone else nearby?"

"No one, Mr. Gander. No one at all." A wicked smile split her face, and she started away from the sofa, trembling lightly, then giving way to giddy laughter.

Gander suddenly realized what he had done. He made a conscious effort not to stand. He had pushed ahead, thinking he knew exactly what to say in spite of, or perhaps because of, this exotic creature with the strange name and the strange eyes and the long black dress in the middle of the day. And now he'd gone and practically accused her of staging her own rescue. He wanted to take her by her smooth white throat and throttle the memory out of her, make her forget everything he'd said.

"I was just thinking out loud," he said flatly, smiling back. "Maybe I've been in features too long."

Natasha stopped laughing. She approached him with her hand out. "I am afraid I have no more time."

"But I'm not finished!" he protested.

"Oh, but you are, Mr. Gander. You are."

"I'll call again. I have this story to write . . ."

"Goodbye, Mr. Gander."

He stood on the third-floor landing, staring at the closed door. He turned and plunged noisily down the two flights to the vestibule, but at the bottom stopped, listening to the hollow, static background noise of the intercom. She was listening to him leave.

Maybe waiting to drop another gourd on him.

He bolted through the door, hopping across the broken gourd on the stoop and skipping down the steps to the street. At his car, the door key in his hand, he looked back. She was at the window, her long body rising in the white-trimmed frame, black hair trailing over the telephone receiver in her raised hand.

He smiled and waved tentatively at the third-floor window. Natasha Nyle ignored him, staring out over the street, her lips moving rapidly into the receiver.

Patty's List

Back in his apartment in the city, at his desk by the living-room window, Gander stared at an empty page, the minutes drifting by.

The further into the past his interview with Natasha Nyle receded, the more it looked like a practical joke. And hers was only the *first* of his interviews.

The minute hand dropped.

The whole interview had been wrong from the start. The way she caught him off guard, sitting so close and touching him, the way he fumbled for words. He knew what had gone wrong; he'd been interviewing people for years. Why hadn't he tried to win her over, gain her confidence, be her friend? Probably because the gourd had thrown him. But the episode with the red eyes hadn't helped either. Those crazy red flashes.

Although his chance to deliver them was forever lost, a dozen opening lines washed around his brain: "I'm here to find out the truth, Miss Nyle"; "Miss Nyle, I'm here because I wanted to hear *your* side"; "Miss Nyle, why *do* you look like a ghost?"

The big assignment, the one he'd waited for.

Another ten minutes slipped away.

· · ·

When the intercom rang, he jumped at the sound, cracking a knee against the edge of his desk. He leaned into the wall, massaging his kneecap, his bared teeth brother to a grin. In an hour and twenty minutes at his desk, he had managed to write "In the dark streets of the Southern Tier" on an empty white page. "Damn intercom," he muttered, hobbling away toward the kitchen speaker.

"Harvey," a woman's voice said, then asked, "it's me?"

"C'mon up," he answered, and only then realized he had no idea whom he had just invited in. Almost instinctively he had assumed it was a neighbor, Melvina, who sometimes dropped by on her way home from work. But though his intercom reception was poor, he realized with growing certainty that it had not been Mel's voice. In fact, he hadn't the slightest idea who was now climbing the stairs to meet him.

In this small pure gap in a world of articulate facts, a latent inarticulate desire welled up within. Perhaps it was the way Natasha Nyle had kept moving beside him on the sofa, but something now stirred deep inside Gander, and he half hoped, beyond all logic, that it was Patty Rose, his office secretary, arriving out of the blue for a visit, simply because he had once asked her out for dinner. An invitation she had turned down flat. And although he knew, with no room for doubt, that she could not possibly be arriving at his door to accept, with a sudden and impulsive change of heart, his invitation, he diverted himself with the notion nonetheless, walking back from the kitchen through the living room and toward the front door, imagining opening it onto her, Patty, her dress in casual disarray, her eyes wet, her hair wild.

He could hear light footsteps on the stairway two flights below as he turned the knob and opened the door. And stood face-to-face with Natasha Nyle, white as death and staring back at him, her head lolling to one side as though she'd just been hanged. She smiled her beautiful smile. Without a word, without a pause, without so much as a flicker of recognition, Gander gently closed the door on the apparition and, alone again in his apartment, stared at the blank white paint on the inside of his front door. He turned the metal knob a second time and opened the door.

Onto Patty. His secretary. Fully dressed and properly composed. But Patty.

In part from sheer surprise, in part from a spasm of guilt, Gander almost shouted at her: "Patty!"

"What's the matter?" she exclaimed.

He brushed past her into the hall and leaned over the banister, looking down the stairs.

"Harvey, what's the *matter*?" she repeated, plainly offended now.

He peered up to the fourth floor before turning back. "Patty," he said, as though by explanation, "did you pass anyone on your way up?"

"I didn't see anybody. Harvey, what is it?" She went to the banister, looking up with him to the fourth floor.

"Nothing, it's nothing," he answered, his voice dropping. "I just thought I saw somebody."

"*Who?*"

"That woman I tried to interview this afternoon. Patty, I just . . . You didn't see a woman?"

"I didn't see *any*one."

"No," he said, looking back through the open door into his vacant apartment. "Neither did I."

"Why don't we go inside?" Patty suggested. "We'll just sit down and take a minute, okay, Harvey? You tell me about it, okay?"

"There's nothing to tell. I didn't see anyone."

"Where didn't you see her?"

He pointed accusingly at her feet. "There! Right there where you're standing!"

"Let's go inside. Okay?"

Gander glanced over his shoulder at the closed door.

"I'd be thrilled," Patty admitted, "if you told me you were just kidding."

He looked at her. "I was just kidding." He looked at the door. He looked at her.

"You worry me," she said.

They sat facing one another in his living room, he in his armchair, she on the sofa.

"So, Patty," Gander offered, seeking some point of reconciliation. "What brings you by?"

She sat up. "I don't believe it. You forgot about my assignment."

"Pardon?"

"I spend half my day, I practically skip lunch, I do all this as a favor to you, and you don't have the slightest idea why I'm even *here*? That's the last . . ."

"Whoa, Patty, wait, wait," Gander interrupted. "I've been trying to write this article and I met this crazy woman and the whole thing . . . I swear I saw her out in the hall. I did not imagine this."

"You don't even know what I'm talking about."

"Of course I do," Gander answered regretfully. "The Superlative Man rescues I asked you to check."

"I mean, I spent half my day," she repeated.

"I was only surprised you came all the way over here," Gander offered, shifting quickly. "But your timing is perfect. I really appreciate it, Patty." He spread his hands admiringly.

"Well, you're on my way home, you know."

"Am I?" Gander leaned toward her. "So tell me. What did you find?"

"I went all the way back in the index to when the Superlative

Man saved that very first woman. Remember? The very first time he saved somebody? But it's never happened before last spring. There never was another time when he had to save two people in two different places at the same time. At least not that anyone ever reported. Since then it's happened four times."

Gander watched her as she spoke, his eyes drifting down the slow landscape of her sweater. He caught himself and looked quickly up. "I thought so," he said. "I mean, that's what I thought."

"I've got four more names for you," she explained, looking away toward the window. For a second he thought she was going to smile, but instead she pulled a piece of white paper and several newspaper clippings from her pocketbook and handed them across the coffee table. She met his eyes and said, "These people were all saved in the double rescues."

Gander read the names, folded the white sheet around the clippings, and slid the packet into his shirt pocket. "If they're as helpful as Natasha Nyle . . ." He started but didn't finish. He stood, looked about the room as though suddenly distracted, and wandered away toward the far window.

Patty eyed him uncertainly, as though unsure whether he expected her to get up and follow. She thought better of it, shook her hair briefly, and slipped off her shoes, propping her feet on the coffee table and leaning back into the sofa. "What a day," she said, her eyes drifting to a near close.

"Want a beer?" Gander asked, looking back from the window.

"I'd love a *drink*."

"Brandy? An aperitif?"

"Oh, high-class."

"Certainly. Something strong? Something sweet? Something vaguely unpronounceable?"

"I thought you were putting me on. What have you got?"

"Scotch."

"That's what I want."

Gander went into the kitchen, opened several cabinets, dropped a glass onto the tile floor without breaking it, and fixed Patty's drink. He pulled a beer from the fridge for himself but poured it too fast, so that it foamed over and spilled down onto the counter. He waited, watching the foam die away.

Patty asked, "How'd the interview go?" She leaned against the door frame, her hair falling down one side of her face. Gander's glance lingered, if only for a moment. Every impulse in his body told him to look at her, and he didn't dare. As surprised as he had been to see her at his door, he knew this was strictly business. So assume nothing. She's here about the articles you made her look up, that's it. He lifted his glass and turned to her. A toast. She reached over to pick up her own and raised it half-heartedly.

"Tired?" he asked.

"Thanks a lot."

"I didn't mean it that way. You look great. But maybe you're tired."

She watched him a second. "I'm beat," she said. "So put it on page one. But you're changing the subject. How'd it go? The woman you interviewed."

"Tried to interview. I think she kicked me out."

"You mean she was polite about it." She sipped her whiskey, set the glass on the counter, and lit a cigarette. Gander had never seen her smoke. He had never seen her do much of anything except answer the phone and shuffle mail, sitting at her desk and nodding hello to the reporters who drifted in and out. "So what happened?" she asked.

"I still don't know. When I got there, I realized I didn't have a clue how to explain to her what I was looking for. I mean, what was I supposed to say? Gee, Miss Nyle, used any good drugs lately?"

"What did you say?"

"I'm not sure exactly, but I guess I told her that the overdoses were tied to the rescues."

"You're kidding."

"Then I told her I thought she'd staged her own rescue."

Patty rolled her eyes.

"No, really. This was straight off the top of my head. But, Patty, she practically admitted to me that she *did* stage it."

"She *told* you that?"

"Maybe not in so many words, but she didn't deny it."

"And then she kicked you out?"

Gander nodded. "I keep thinking about Martin," he said, "and how if he were here he'd probably have this story already. Me? I get kicked out."

Patty shifted slightly but leaned back into the door frame. "I saw Martin's obituary in the paper this morning," she said. "Harvey, can I be honest with you?"

Gander flinched.

"I know you were upset when you wrote it, but I'm surprised York let that go to print."

"He liked it. He told me he liked it."

"If you say so. He could just as easily have fired you."

"Fired me for what?"

"For turning in an all-out assault on the Superlative Man."

"It wasn't *about* the Superlative Man. It was about Martin. And besides, York liked it."

"I find that hard to believe," she assured him.

Gander looked out the window at the street, concluding once and for all that Patty had not knocked on his apartment door in search of love.

"What else happened in the interview?" she asked.

"I talked too much. Even if she doesn't look like she just rose from a grave, which she does, I still didn't need to . . ."

"I thought she was beautiful."

"She is beautiful. She's also white like a ghost. So I start telling this woman who's got on a long black dress and has skin that looks like smoke, I start telling her about the connection between the overdoses and the rescues, and suddenly she clams up and denies there's any conspiracy, says it's all a big coincidence."

"What are you talking about, a conspiracy?"

"I don't know what I'm talking about, but I started thinking that maybe all those double rescues were staged."

"What for?"

"To make the Superlative Man look bad, I suppose, because then he'd be stuck trying to save two people at the same time. But I was just warming up to this when all of a sudden she practically admits it. Then she stands up and tells me to leave."

"Are you *sure*?"

"About the phony rescues? Not really, but something's up, and she's either in on it or she knows a whole lot about it. And York wanted something from me tonight."

"So give him something."

"Patty, why *me*? If somebody's out to get the Superlative Man, why should *I* save him? I don't *want* this story."

"Harvey, this is real news."

"I don't *want* to write about the Superlative Man," he repeated, his voice rising. And suddenly he was shouting. "Doesn't anyone ever get tired of this Superlative Man thing? Can't they ever once just for*get* about him!"

"It was Martin's obituary that started this," she said, eyeing him. "You better watch out, fella."

He turned away to the window. "All I ever wanted was a news story, but I never asked for this. And now I don't have anything to hand in to Paul York."

"So I'll get going and you can get to work." Her voice changed, as though she'd said too much, or said it too hard. She stayed, leaning into the door frame. "The woman you interviewed, Natasha Nyle, was she the one you thought you saw out in the hallway?"

"The one and only."

"Call York and ask for an extension, Harvey."

"I can't."

"Tell him you need more time. Tell him anything, but call him."

"I *can't.*"

"*Call* him," she insisted and turned and lifted the telephone receiver from the wall beside her. She held it out.

Gander raised his hands in resignation, walked back across the kitchen, and took the receiver from her outstretched hand. She turned to the phone and dialed.

"York?" Gander said into the receiver after a pause. "It's me, Gander."

"Yeah," Gander answered. "I went down to High Water."

"Right."

"Well, not too much, you know. It didn't seem like much of a story."

"Wait a minute, York."

"No, wait."

"York! Will you *listen* to me?"

"I'd like to do a little more poking around."

"Yeah, I interviewed a girl out in the borough."

"Natasha Nyle."

"Because I got a feeling, that's all."

"So what about putting it back a day or two?"

"No, no. No more." And then, his eyes lifting to Patty's, "Yeah?"

"Okay, okay, I know you don't like to do it. Don't worry. I'll get you a story."

And he hung up.

"So there," Patty said.

"I don't think he was too happy about it."

"What difference does that make?"

"And I had this funny feeling he knew who Natasha Nyle was."

"Forget Paul York." She set her empty glass on the counter. "Look, I have to go, but keep me posted, okay?" She turned, and Gander followed her through the living room to the front door, but she waited before opening it. "Are you sure you're okay, Harvey? I mean that business in the hall and all?"

"I'm fine. I promise."

Back in the kitchen the intercom buzzer rang.

"Company," Patty said, and smiled. "Maybe it's your friend Natasha."

"My good friend Natasha."

"What do you think, Harvey? Should I sneak out a back stairway?" She eyed Gander from under one raised brow. "I mean, now that the next young woman in line is obviously waiting to come up."

"But of course," Gander answered, following her lead. "And if you wouldn't mind, could you sneak up to the fourth floor? Then, when she comes into my apartment, I'll close the door behind her and you can slip away home free."

"Harvey, it's brilliant!" Patty rejoined, but still waited, her hand on the knob. "You make me wonder, though. You sort of leave the impression that you're an old hand at this, and I'm not sure if you're honestly teasing me or just pretending to tease me."

"*Me?*" Gander protested, one hand flat against his chest, his eyes wide under high brows.

So that Patty could not resist getting in the last jab. "And don't worry about the Natasha Nyle interview. You've got four more."

Back in the kitchen, the intercom buzzer rang long, twice.

"Scram, will you? She's getting impatient."

" 'Bye, Harvey." Patty waved slightly and started away down the stairs.

Gander closed the door on her and headed back to the kitchen. "Hello?" he said into the intercom speaker.

"Police," a sullen voice answered. "Open up."

Plainclothesmen

Heavy footsteps climbed the stairs. Gander waited in his open doorway, listening. Two men. They would have passed Patty on her way out, maybe held the door for her. Below him, on the second-floor landing, they turned into the next flight, and Gander thought he heard a low voice say, "So who's the girl?"

They came into view. Plainclothesmen, one a touch shorter and thicker, the other only slightly taller, narrow and lean. The shorter man locked black eyes on Gander the moment he turned the corner, the taller man beside him watching his feet, not looking up until the final step and the landing. The three men faced each other in a tight triangle.

"Gander," the shorter man said.

"That's right," Gander acknowledged.

"Right," the taller man allowed. "And we're the police. Mind if we come in?" But he started past Gander without waiting for an answer, the shorter man walking deliberately after him and glancing at Gander as he passed. Gander brought up the rear, following and saying, "C'mon in," but leaving the hall door open behind.

No one sat down and Gander didn't offer, the three men poised again in a tight triangle in the middle of his living room. The two plainclothesmen studied the room, the taller man's eyes settling first on the closed door into the kitchen, then the hallway down to the bedroom, and lingering there.

It was the shorter man who spoke. "Been here long?" he asked.

"A few years," Gander answered.

"Today. Been here long today?"

"Oh," Gander said. "I thought you meant how long have I lived here."

They waited, watching him.

"A few hours, I guess," Gander concluded.

"You been to the Outer Borough," the shorter man stated.

"Why?" Gander countered.

"Why—because I asked you."

"I just wondered how you knew."

"We knew. So we knew," the taller man explained, then requested, "so talk to us."

"I was in the Outer Borough, yes."

"And you saw Natasha Nyle," the shorter man continued.

Gander nodded, tentatively.

"Answer him," the taller man snapped.

"Yes, okay, yes. What's going on?"

"What time?" the shorter man resumed.

"I don't know. Two, I suppose."

"How long'd you stay?"

"Not very long. Half an hour maybe."

"And then straight home?"

"Yes. What's happened?"

"You left her there?"

"*Yes.*"

"Seen her since?"

Gander paused. Then, more slowly, "No."

"He saw her," the taller man interrupted.

"Shut up," the shorter man shot back. "You just shut up." Then, to Gander, he inquired, "Haven't seen her, huh?"

"I left her in the Outer Borough."

"Okay, now, listen. We're looking for her. We have questions we'd like to ask her. You understand?"

"Because we want to talk to her," the taller man added, looking furtively across his shoulder at his partner, who stared back at him with contempt and who kept staring at him even as he continued speaking to Gander. "We want to talk to her."

Gander said, "I haven't seen her."

The taller man moved slowly sideways, away from his partner, stretching the triangle. "You're a reporter," he informed Gander, stepping back, just out of reach of the shorter man, and then stopping. "Whacha writin'," he asked, "about Nyle?"

"I was interviewing her because the Superlative Man rescued her."

The two plainclothesmen watched one another now as though Gander weren't there.

"You let me know, okay?" the shorter man said to his taller partner, and it took Gander a moment to realize that the words were directed at him. "You let me know if you see her."

"It's just not real likely," Gander explained.

"But you'll let me know," the shorter man repeated to his partner.

"I'm supposed to call you?" Gander asked.

The two men swiveled together to look at him. The shorter man said, "Don't worry, we'll find you." And without further ceremony they turned and walked back through the open front door, the shorter man leading, the taller man following, across the landing and down the stairs, around the corner and out of sight, their footsteps landing heavily, rising oddly back up the stairwell.

Carousel

Gander looked out his kitchen window at the street. The clock on the stove behind him said five after six. It would be light for nearly three more hours.

Down by the curb near the newsstand a platinum blonde in a black cigarette of a dress and red high heels paced the curb, watching the street as though waiting for a cab. One approached from about a block away, but as it pulled over to pick her up, she waved it away, turning and walking back up to the newsstand. Talking to the man inside and Gander could imagine the exchange. Smiling George, the neighborhood newsboy. Answering the girl's questions. Telling her about the town if she was a tourist. Making her wait for her change if she decided to buy something after all. His routine. Then at the last moment dropping it on her like raw egg: Hey, wait! I *reck*ognize you. I seen you! I can't be*leeve* it. (The woman turns back, looking over her shoulder.) No, it *can't* be, George putters on. Was you in *Midnight Pussycat*? (It invariably hooks an uncertain "Excuse me?") *Hey There, Soldier*? (At which the woman stares or, more often, turns and walks away, George gently tossing his last after her.) *Tickle Me Fancy*?

Not really funny. But most men laughed and some women

flushed. And George kept at it, telling the occasional cop who pursued it, "But I thought I *reck*ognized her!" Gander had seen him do this to a few girls, and the first time he'd laughed, too. The second time he felt sorry for the girl. By the third time he was bored. But George had been at it for years. It'd be no small job doing a feature on him:

> Passing out dailies to the passing throngs for a generation, George has become a neighborhood fixture. A newsboy, sure. But he's more than that: a tourist guide, a raconteur, a mine of information about a city that's grown up and transformed the landscape all around him. And they say he's famous for his memory. While hints that he's a ladies' man don't keep the pretty girls away, he never forgets a one.

It wouldn't be the first feature on some old newsstand hound. All he had to do was sit behind his counter for twenty years and, wham! Destiny! His face looking up from every bathroom floor in the city.

He sat at his kitchen table leaning over the evening edition of the *Metropolitan Meteor*. A pigeon landed on the window ledge and glanced inside, then strutted into flight. Gander got up and walked back over to the window to look down at the street. Near the newsstand a passing couple paused on the sidewalk. The man went up to the recessed counter and returned a moment later with a paper under his arm. They walked away. The blond woman was nowhere to be seen. The street was quiet. The small sound was coming from his living room.

The swinging door into the living room was closed. A shadow moved in the empty line at the base. He scanned the kitchen counter: a frying pan on the stove. He stepped gingerly toward it and lifted it straight from the burner, carried it raised like a sign and kicked open the door. It swung out and sprang back against him, knocking the frying pan out of his hand and across the tiled floor.

But he had seen it. There on the living-room floor. He pushed the swinging door gently open.

And it meowed.

A little shock of a thing. A tiny puzzle of black and white, with hair that stood straight out. Crouched on the carpet, it seemed frightened, working its mouth: M'ow. M'ow. High, quick dots of sound. All exclamation and no song. Gander picked it up, and its four paws' claws stretched into his shirt. Across the room his front door stood half a foot ajar. Just inside it, a small cardboard box lay spilled over on its side. He looked down at the kitten pressed against his chest, thinking, So, you're a special delivery, are you? He walked over to pick up the box, but as he lifted it from the floor with his free hand, a piece of paper and a stone fell out: a white envelope floated to the carpet, his name scrawled across the front in Violet's hand, and, thumping on the carpet beside it, the little stone man he had seen on Natasha Nyle's coffee table stared back up with its strange red eyes.

The kitten sat on the kitchen table in the bright sunshine, leaning over a white saucer of milk, steadily lapping. Gander stood at the kitchen window. The blond woman had reappeared and, with her back to him, stood looking into the newsstand. His face felt tight, or maybe it was the muscles beneath his face. He reread the single scrap of white paper in his hand.

Dear Harvey,
I shouldn't have said anything last night. Jeannie heard me, I think. Nobody is supposed to know about the Harem, tho

maybe she didn't hear that part. It's just I don't have anyone to talk to down here. Nobody at all. But they think you're working on a story and I'm afraid now because of what happened. Can you meet me by the carousel around 7:30?

Love,
Violet

Gander looked up from the letter just in time to see the blonde stagger back from the newsstand as though she'd been shoved. She turned and stared directly at him. He drew back. She was a dead ringer for Violet Hayes. There were a dozen windows around him. She could be looking at any of them. She wasn't. She was looking at him.

A low black coupe with red lines pulled up short in front of her. She hadn't signaled. She didn't move. The passenger door swung open, a man's sleeved arm reaching out, beckoning. She looked back over her shoulder into George's stand. She looked up at Gander. She turned and walked to the cab, disappearing under the black roof. The car accelerated away from the curb, passed under Gander's window, rounded a corner, and was gone.

Standing in his building's vestibule beside mailboxes and a panel of intercom buttons, he looked out at the empty street through a single clear pane in a patchwork of frosted glass. He tipped his hat, shielding his eyes against the late-day sun reflecting in the windows across the street. His left arm bent at the elbow and his left hand held an edge of his buttoned jacket. Underneath the jacket the kitten lay cradled in the crook of his arm, its claws still fastened to his shirt. But it seemed to be sleeping. His right hand burrowed between his jacket buttons and scratched its tiny forehead.

He crossed the street and walked down the opposite sidewalk, approaching the newsstand from its side, the racks of magazines and newspapers flaring like a fan until the whole face of the newsstand lay open before him and he stared at the man inside.

He said: "Where's George." It was a statement: George is not here.

A dark, mop-haired, sullen-jowled man stared back at him. "Wha'd'ya want? A paper? Buy a paper."

"Where's George?"

"Maybe he took a day off. Maybe he's on vacation. Maybe he retired."

"Who are you?"

"The Superlative Man. Wha'd'ya want? A paper?"

"Where's *George*?"

"Move on, bud."

M'ow.

The man looked at Gander's jacket. He looked at Gander. "George who?"

Gander turned slowly, his feet planted, looking over his shoulder to his third-floor windows. He turned back to the man inside. "Somebody who used to work here." He set a five on the counter and picked up an evening *Mercury*.

"Nothin' smaller?"

Gander shook his head.

"Suits you."

Two blocks away on Carnival Street, across from the park, Gander closed the door of a green metal-and-glass telephone booth and dialed the *Metropolitan Meteor*.

"Elmo Jade," he said. "City."

Jade was a city news reporter with a reputation for knowing people and a knack for weaving rumors into the kind of breaking story other papers spent a lot of money chasing down. At the *Metropolitan Meteor*, a small pond compared to the *Daily Mercury*, he was a big bullfrog, and Jack Fowler, the news editor, was more than happy to let him go his own way. The *Metropolitan Meteor* was fine. Everybody agreed about that. But Jade was better. Yet year after year he stayed on, collecting his paycheck. Why he stayed was one of the little mysteries of the profession.

Jade and Gander worked on different floors on opposite sides of the building, and Gander rarely saw him, barely knew him. But Martin Gale used to talk about Jade not as though he worked in News but as though he were News. Over the years Gander had come to think of Jade as the essence of the first section, a sort of reigning genius; and if it hadn't been for his creeping unease about the way this day was going, one thing after another jumping at him like headlines, he never would have called.

"What is it."

"Jade. Harvey Gander. Features?"

"Sure, I know you. What's up?"

"I think I'm in trouble."

"Where are you?"

"On Carnival, across the street from the park."

"Go inside the park, a few benches up from the gates. Halfway between the gates and the carousel."

"And do what?"

"Give me fifteen minutes."

In the city archives nobody called it Carnival Park. In the city archives they thought it was named after some guy nobody outside the archives had ever heard of. But fifty years earlier, in the heyday of carnival life, the name Carnival Park had fastened and stuck. The name no longer made any sense. Now people walked into Carnival Park to escape the sideshows outside it, and only a single carousel lingered, in a copse not far from the Carnival Street entrance. But habits of speech are habits of mind, and at least this last carousel was an original, with a double circle of wild horses. Every night after dark, on through the summer, it came to glaring life.

Across the street from the phone booth, wrought iron gates opened in the low stone wall wrapping the park. When you stood at the gates, a herringbone brick walk curved away toward the trees, and a single bench marked the edge of a wood. From the bench Gander had a view of the gates out to the street and of the carousel, nestled deep in the trees.

It was still only seven-twenty. The merry-go-round wouldn't wind up until eight. Gander waited, the evening *Mercury* spread on his lap. He glanced back and forth between the shuttered-up carousel and the street. In the high-rise apartments overlooking the park, in the repeating rows of three- and four-story brownstones stretching away across the city, people finished their dinners, read newspapers, sat on stoops.

A long lamppost of a man stood in profile between the gate pillars, his face turned into the park. Gander nodded, his hat brim dipping. Elmo Jade touched his own brim and started up the path, his jacket open, his hands in his trouser pockets, his stride unhurried, deliberate.

He stood over six feet tall in his hat, his jacket, draped behind his wrists at his hips, emphasizing his narrow frame and wide shoulders, his narrow face and wide hat making a pattern to match. His tie, light brown like his baggy suit, hung loose at his throat, and his face, shadowed and withdrawn, a long line accented by nose and chin, somehow seemed continuous with the tie.

Gander slid over and Jade slipped to the empty slats beside him. The kitten, still fastened to Gander's shirt, peered with one eye past the upturned lapel. Jade looked at the little creature.

"Don't tell me," he said. "It's illegitimate."

Gander grimaced. He had meant to smile, but at that moment the kitten shifted.

Something jangled near the carousel. The two men looked over. A caretaker was lifting away one of the large wooden screens that, like a series of gates, concealed the horses. Between each pair of outside support poles all around the carousel, these wide wooden screens of narrow crisscrossed slats stood flush with the outer edge of the carousel floor. Every night the caretaker had to lift each one of them away, unlocking a loop of chain in the first and then carrying them off, one at a time, to lean against a nearby fence. He'd do this until he had a standing rack of a dozen or so of the wooden frames and the carousel horses stood fully exposed. Gander had watched it before. When the caretaker was through, he'd turn on colored lights, crank up a music box, and start the horses spinning.

From where Gander and Jade sat, the first horses appeared just to the right, off center, the man lifting the first tall screen out of its grooves and carrying it before him like a wall. They watched him feel his way with his feet as he neared the fence and then set the screen on the ground. He turned, went back for the next frame, and began to work his way around toward the back. Before long he would reappear on the other side, working his way toward the front.

"You were the first person I thought of," Gander said, still watching the caretaker. He turned to Jade. "But don't ask me why."

"What's up?"

"I don't know. I maybe stumbled onto something."

"And?"

"Then things took a bad turn."

"Bad ain't good," Jade coaxed.

"I'm on a series about some overdoses downtown."

"I know," Jade said.

Gander looked up from the bricks. "I didn't think anybody knew."

"They don't," Jade admitted. "But I heard about it."

"I drove to the Outer Borough to do an interview."

"Who?"

"Some woman named Natasha Nyle, and it didn't go too well, but when I got home I thought I saw her outside my apartment door. A little later I see some blonde down on the street, and she looks familiar. Turns out it was Violet Hayes, a woman I saw down at High Water last night. And I don't know exactly when, but she left a box inside my door with this in it." He lifted the little stone man from his jacket pocket and held it out in the evening light, then slid it back under his pocket flap. "Earlier today it was in Natasha Nyle's apartment. I look out the window again and this blonde looks up at me and it *is* Violet, but she's got on this nutty wig and right then a car pulls up and they make her get into it. When I go downstairs to ask the newsboy across the street if she'd said anything to him—he's been there for years—he's gone and some goon's in his place. You could stake out my building from that newsstand if you wanted."

The caretaker was circling back into view. They watched him carry the next wooden frame away from the carousel, on his way to the fence.

"I remember Violet," Jade said. "A blond wig?"

"Platinum. And a skinny black dress and red high heels."

At first Jade said nothing. Then his eyes darkened and he said, "No."

It took Gander a moment to register. Jade was not talking to him. He stared past Gander's shoulder at the carousel.

The caretaker had arrived at the last section of crisscrossed fence, front and center, and lifted it from its guide holes. He was carrying it away like a great shield to the fence, unaware of what he had exposed to the two men on the park bench a little way down the path. He set the fence section on the ground, let it land against the other sections with a tap, and turned.

Nothing moved. The caretaker, the two men on the park bench, the carousel, the empty sky.

When the caretaker collapsed, dropping to his knees, his hands rising to his face. Jade shot off the bench and a moment later stood over him, clutching a handful of hair and yanking back the man's head, the body twisting beneath, the face horrified and looking at the sky.

A dozen claws penetrated Gander's chest. He left the bench, walking toward the carousel. Jade slipped to his side, fast and silent, gripping his upper arm.

"Far enough."

Beneath the raised, frozen-in-prancing legs of a carved wooden horse, under a tossed mane and bared teeth, sprawled the body of Violet Hayes, broken like a toy, arms and legs angling across the floorboards. One hand gripped the horse's metal support pole. A blond wig lay separated from her head and spread away from her face like a crazy halo, her red-painted lips drawn back tight, her eyes glassy and wide, her black cigarette dress yanked down past her shoulders. She still had on one red high heel.

Jade growled: "Go. Call the cops."

"Violet," Gander whispered.

"Was there anyone else in the car? You said she left the newsstand in a car."

"I don't know. Yes. A man. I didn't see him." His hand reached under his jacket impulsively. The kitten cried, squirming. "Jade, she looked at my window."

"I know. I know. Gander, why did you *call* me?"

"I told you, I don't know. Because I saw her leave in that car. Because they were heading away from the park."

Jade knelt on the carousel floor, touching her open throat. His dark eyes swung down the path.

A noise like carnival music melted into voices. Gander raised his head. Approaching up the walkway at a rapid pace, the caretaker muttered unintelligibly between two burly blue-uniformed cops. The cops stared straight ahead as they walked, talking to each other over the head of the caretaker. Each had a hand on his holstered gun.

Gander sat hunched on the carousel floor, his elbows on his knees, his head hanging between his shoulders. "You were too rough on that guy," he said.

"I wanted to know if he was acting," Jade said. "If he already knew."

"And?"

"I don't think so."

The Coffee Shop

Circus music followed as Gander and Jade walked out through the gates of the park. Gander waited on the sidewalk, looking back at the carousel lights shining up through the treetops into the night. A crowd milled around outside the roped-off merry-go-round, and policemen stood inside, talking quietly to one another among the horses.

Jade said, "Walk me past your place, past the newsstand."

They crossed Carnival Street and started down Seventh. Two blocks south they passed Gander's stoop and he opened his mouth to speak.

"No," Jade said, his lips not moving. "Keep walking."

The newsstand across the street approached, flared like a fan, and passed. Gander glanced swiftly but again heard the voice. "Don't look. Walk."

A block and a half past the newsstand they turned right onto Cutler. Halfway to Eighth they stopped in the square light of a coffee-shop window.

"That was the man in the newsstand?" Jade asked.

"You told me not to look."

"Your eyes glued to your face?"

Gander said nothing.

"Forget it," Jade said. "Dark curly hair, thick-lipped, clean-shaven, heavy brows, blue work shirt, closed at the collar, black vest."

"The same."

"Have you eaten? You hungry?"

"No. Wet."

"Wet?"

"The cat just peed on my shirt."

Gander pulled the kitten from under his jacket and held it out in the light.

The meal passed without talk. Gander ordered food, and two poached eggs stared at him as he smoked cigarettes and drank coffee, until finally he pushed the plate of corned-beef hash to the side of the table. Jade ate pork chops and mashed potatoes in a pool of stewed tomatoes, then sipped at a cup of black coffee. He drew on a cigarette, blue smoke lingering above the booth.

They sat in the rear of an empty, white-bright coffee shop, the front door locked now, a waitress leaning over the counter beside a cash register, working a pencil through a stack of receipts. On the red bench cushion, the kitten lay curled on newspaper in a small cardboard box, about the size of a shoe box. It said "24 SALT 24" on the side.

"Where I met you," Jade said. "You ever go there?"

"No," Gander answered. "I was wondering about you."

"Sometimes I go by there. But I didn't kill her." Jade sipped his coffee.

"I know," Gander answered. "There wasn't enough time."

"So who knew we were going there?"

"Maybe it was a coincidence," Gander suggested.

"No such thing," said Jade.

"What's that supposed to mean?"

"Did you call me before or after you killed her, Gander?"

Gander stared back. "You listen to me, Jade. This was no setup. I had nothing to do with it."

"Then why did you call me?"

Gander protested: "You've got to *believe* me. I don't even know how I got mixed up in this."

"Me neither, except you called me. How well did you know Violet?"

"I used to know her a little," Gander lied.

Jade stared back at him, his eyes alert and concentrated into little black points, Gander thinking: *I should tell him. I should tell him about Violet's letter.* Instinctively he recoiled, his mind racing: *He'll think I did it. He'll think I killed her. Who knew about the letter?*

Gander said, "I swear I feel like I do when I wake up in the night."

Jade exhaled, studying him.

Gander moved uncomfortably in his seat. "Do you believe in evil, Jade?"

"Why not. Look around."

"No, I mean real, like you can touch it."

"Or maybe it can touch you," Jade reflected. "Most people never think about it, never look around. Ask them and they'll say they don't know what you're talking about. Ask them and they'll look at you like you're dreamy, like it's a lot of hooey, like it's philosophy. Then one day, like everybody else, they catch a whiff in the same room and they know it. And that, my friend, is one of life's defining moments."

"You know something, Jade? You're a very reassuring man to talk to. I tell you, I feel better already."

"Hey, if you believe in evil, you can always believe in good, too."

"Oh, well, there you go."

"And then there's always the Superlative Man," Jade considered. He signaled for more coffee. "All right, now *you* listen," he said. "I think I believe you. Maybe this was a setup. But you've got to come through for me. Go back. Tell me what happened in the Outer Borough."

For the next few minutes Gander's voice droned on alone in the back of the restaurant, until Jade barked, *"What?"* and the waitress looked up from her receipts. The kitten arched its back, stretching on the newspaper. Jade immediately lowered his voice. "Gander, you told her *what?*"

"I didn't know what else to say. So I told her the overdoses had all been rescued by the Superlative Man."

Jade shrugged. "I don't believe it."

"I had to have *some* reason for being there."

"And? What did she say?"

"She told me it was no conspiracy."

"Is that when she threw you out?"

"No, she threw me out when I accused her of phonying her own rescue."

Jade blew smoke at Gander's poached eggs. "You are one piece of work, you know that?"

"Jade, I was thinking out loud."

"Why do you talk so much?"

"I had no way of knowing. None. If this was such a hot story, then why did I get it? Why Features and not News?"

"I happen to be interested in that question myself. But so far nobody's giving me any answers. Believe me, if I knew you were going to walk around playing Show and Tell, you would've heard from me before I heard from you."

"I don't believe this. I don't even know why I called you. The interview with Natasha Nyle was rotten luck, okay?"

Jade eyed him with distaste. "Yeah," he said. "Rotten luck for Violet Hayes, too."

"I saw her last night," Gander said quietly.

"Violet? Where?"

"I told you, High Water. York gave me a list of the overdoses and I recognized one of the names. A guy named Albert Long."

"You knew him?"

"Not really, but I used to hang out down there before it changed hands and I'd see him sometimes."

"So you went down to check it out?"

Gander nodded.

"And you saw Violet?"

"I ran into her and we talked."

"What'd she tell you?"

"On the level?"

"Always," Jade answered.

"I mean between us? I can trust you on this?"

"You called me, Gander."

"She told me all the overdoses had been rescued by the Superlative Man."

"And you turned around and announced this to Natasha Nyle?"

Gander was silent.

"Did Violet tell you to check out the double rescues, too?"

"No, that was me needing a place to start. I mean, what the hell do I have to give Paul York? So far, about nothing."

"Gander, so far you've got a slew of overdoses, every one of them rescued by the Superlative Man. You've got some conspiracy, and you've got a girl dead on the floor of a merry-go-round."

"Thanks for the headlines. Now what am I supposed to do with it?"

"I didn't say you were ready to print. I'm only saying you covered a lot of ground in twenty-four hours."

"But, Jade, how does it fit together? Why was she *killed*?" Gander's left hand trembled and he slid it under the table.

"Maybe because you talk too much."

"They killed her because of *me*?"

"What do you think, ace?"

Gander slammed the table with the palm of his right hand and shouted, "It was just a bloody conversation in a *bar*." But his voice fell. "They should never have killed her, Jade."

Jade tapped an ash from his cigarette. It floated to the floor. "What did York tell you?"

"More questions," Gander said and sank back against the cushion. "He said Martin Gale had been on the story so he thought of me. He wondered if I'd follow up on the overdoses. That's about all."

"And you checked them?"

"I had one of the girls at the office look at them. Patty. What are you getting at?"

"I wrote a lead on those overdoses, checked out every one of the people on York's list. Nobody but Martin Gale picked up on it. You with me now?"

"No."

"If York's so interested in the story, why doesn't he just go to the file, pull my lead, and call me?"

"I didn't ask him."

"Gander, what does he think of you as a reporter?"

"You know damn well what he must think of me. This is the first shot I've had at anything. He's got me shelved. Strictly features."

"So why assign it to you?"

"Maybe he doesn't think it's much of a story."

"Maybe he doesn't want it to be."

The waitress stood at the edge of the table holding a half-filled pot of coffee. "A couple of minutes, guys, okay?"

"Mary," Jade said. "You know this neighborhood. Where's the paperboy from up the street?"

"George," Gander added.

Mary looked at the picture window. "Got me. He's been there ever since I came on."

"Today?"

"Nah, seventeen years ago."

"He isn't there now," Jade explained.

"You haven't seen him?" Gander asked.

"George is a dirty old man," she answered. "Maybe he got smart and retired, gave the world a break. Coffee?"

"Maybe she's right," Gander thought out loud when she was gone.

"Yeah? Then why'd you call me?"

"I said maybe."

"And maybe you've been dreaming. And maybe that little stone carving in your pocket isn't really there. Maybe I'm wasting time talking to you."

"Jade, did York give me the job because I couldn't do it?"

"Maybe."

"But why?"

"Maybe he thought some people would scare easy if they thought a story might get done. Makes York look like a man to reckon with."

"I called him earlier today."

"What about?"

"Needing more time."

"And?"

"Time, boys," Mary called over. "I'm going home."

"I got a couple extra days."

"Doesn't fit. What'd you tell him?"

"He didn't want to at first. So I told him I wanted to do some more checking into this Natasha Nyle. I told him I thought I was on to a story."

"Man, you got a big mouth."

"All right, boys," Mary stood over the table. "Bedtime."

Out on the sidewalk, ill lit now with the restaurant window dark, Jade wrote two telephone numbers on the back of a business card. Gander studied the card, the salt box tucked under his arm. "You can get me," Jade explained, "anytime. But don't mention my name. To anyone. Ever. As far as anybody's concerned, and I mean York or whoever you sleep with or anybody, I'm not in on this."

"What if we've been seen together? We *have* been seen together."

"Can't be helped."

"But what am I supposed to do about the rest of the interviews? I have all these other names."

"Keep doing them. But shut up and let them do the talking. You're interviewing them. Nobody expects you to talk."

"I'm way over my head."

"You are," Jade agreed. "But I'll tell you something." He dipped his hand into his pocket and looked back over his shoulder at the darkened window. "So am I. But as long as you know it and I know it, then we'll take it one step at a time. Just keep your eyes open and your mouth shut. And if you ever call me at work, do not say your name." He started away down the sidewalk, Gander calling after him.

"Jade."

He looked back sideways.

"You don't believe in coincidence?"

Jade said, "Things don't happen for no reason."

A few blocks away a siren wailed. The kitten moved, tilting the salt box.

"Then why did I call you?"

Jade watched him a moment. Then his hand lifted from his

jacket pocket, tossing a dark lozenge through the air. Gander caught it at his shoulder and stared into the shadowed face of the little stone man, his hand dropping automatically to his own jacket pocket.

It was there.

There were two of the little carvings.

But Jade's brown suit was drifting away into the night.

In the middle of the night, a single light bulb burning, Gander sat alone in his living room, unable to sleep, unable to rise out of his chair. Violet, too, gone now. His hands gripped the armrests, the anger coursing through him like a chemical change.

Dime

Morning light.

Listen.

Gander lifted his head from the wet pillow, tossed back his sheet, and moved swiftly to the door. Only then he hesitated, watching his hand on the knob, turning. But when he opened the door, the room was still, the furniture in its place, the picture of his parents staring back. Something rustled behind him. The kitten sat up at the foot of his bed, yawning, in his shoe.

It had started with a voice in the living room and he'd glided away in the dark to the open door. A lamp lay knocked over on the floor, its shade angling to spotlight his parents. There, nailed into the face of the picture, the kitten writhed in the light. Off in the shadows the front door closed with a click, footsteps pounding down the stairs, a woman's voice howling up the stairwell.

Not a good dream.

His thumb and forefinger wound his watch. He unbuckled the strap and set it beside the lamp on his bedside table. He picked it up to look at the time. Seven-twenty.

·   ·   ·

He drank hot coffee in gulps at the kitchen window, watching a trashman heave an empty can at an alley wall. The man turned and ran, the can flying.

On the windowsill in the sun, his slippered feet sat propped between a stained saucer and an ashtray, the newspaper in his lap, the front page up:

CAROUSEL CRIME!
BLONDE SPRAWLED
UNDER WOODEN HORSE

The square white scrap of Violet's letter angled out from beneath the paper, and the list of names Patty had given him lay unfolded in his hand. He silently read the list of four names, imagining rooms, backdrops highlighting conjured faces.

He leaned into the window frame, exactly as he had the day before when Violet stood down by the newsstand. He plunged his hands into the pockets of his bathrobe, his mouth hanging slack, and stared into the sunshine, seeing her terrified grin, her thin body all angles on the carousel floor. *I'll tell him about the letter and he'll think I did it. They all will.* Rereading the names in his hand. *But they know. The people on this list. They know who killed her.*

He glanced at the first name as he dialed, the receiver pressed against his ear, and listened to the line connect, the first ring, the second.
  "What is it?"
  "Mr. Dime?"
  "Dime, yeah."
  "Harvey Gander. I'm with the *Metropolitan Meteor* and I'd like

to interview you in connection with a series on people saved by the Superlative Man?"

"The Superlative Man."

"I've got the right Mr. Dime?"

"You got the right to what?"

"No. I mean, you're the right person? You were saved by the Superlative Man?"

"Yeah, sure. Wait a minute."

Low voices muttering. A woman was speaking, saying something that sounded like "night sky." But it could have been background interference. Or maybe Gander was imagining things again, hearing voices in the oil-spatter static of a crowded telephone line, a thought that sent him wandering past the kitten on his wall, by the woman on the stairs, and out into everything that had happened in the last twenty-four hours. Was this what it was like to lose your mind? It just wanders away? A prodigal sanity? And you watch it go, saying to yourself, Is this what it's like to lose your mind?

"Yes," the man's voice answered clearly.

"What," Gander said.

"You want an interview, you said."

"I do. I know it's late . . ."

"Today's fine."

"This morning?"

"In an hour. Lobby of the Grand."

"I appreciate . . ."

But the line was dead.

Four blocks away from the Grand Hotel, Gander took a shortcut down a side street of fruit stands and haberdashers. Hat shops and shoe shines crouched under painted signs. Hand-lettered awnings knocked caps off delivery boys. Cars and delivery trucks hugged the curbs, and a single line of traffic crept down the middle of the street. A small crowd huddled in front of a radio shop, crammed in between an umbrella stand and a button hole. A speaker blared overhead. Gander stopped to listen.

Inside the window the owner had displayed his best radios—the new Silver Escort Console front and center—and a scattered collection of records. Off to one side, propped on a music stand over the words *Now Playing* was the dust jacket for Volume XV of "Crimes and Accidents: True Recordings from Police Radio." The jacket showed a drawing of the Superlative Man standing on the edge of a skyscraper, watching over the city.

The record was already over a month old. Like the rest of the Police Radio series, it consisted entirely of cops yakking back and forth over the wire about suspects and vehicles and perpetrators, half in fraternity code and half in telegraphese, with a nickname for everyone, including the Superlative Man. They called him Night Light, though nobody seemed to know where the name came from or what it meant.

Gander watched the men and women watching the window. A voice over the speaker pattered on: *"Five ladder connected to the third-floor window. Fireman inside and we got no contact. Wait, that's a gunshot. We hear gunshots. Three officers down behind their cars. Suspect last seen on fire escape outside floor eight. Repeat, floor eight. That's the top. We need backup on next building. Watch the roof. Bulletin. Night Light on roof. We've spotted Night Light. Repeat. He's on the roof. We can see him. He's got the suspect. He's waving the gun. Suspect disarmed. Repeat. Suspect disarmed."*

The little gathering outside the radio shop cheered. Two old men shook hands. Gander shook his head and walked away down the sidewalk, on his way to the Grand Hotel.

The gloomy expanse of the Grand's once-gilded lobby glimmered feebly, its great bauble-dripping chandeliers pocked with dark bulbs and the surviving lights, like wind-pestered candles, trembling and scattering a greasy sheen on red and green furniture, dark, overstuffed, and heavy, and blocking passages through the immense room. Reflections of old age. Wearied grandeur.

It was a commonplace in metropolitan guidebooks to compare entering the lobby of the Grand to stepping back in time, and one week Gander had written up a guide to the guidebooks for the Sunday paper. But only now, standing in the lobby of the Grand for the first time in years, did he see how far the notion bore meaning. On a short rise of steps, looking out over the lobby across the wide carpets and bulky herds of furniture to the long, polished sweep of the front desk, he took a notepad from his jacket pocket and started jotting:

Entering revolving doors like entering dowager's mind—news of day still current in tiny newsstand near front door and outside world—hundreds of people wander through lobby, voices circulating, a soft drone in humid air—what goes on in a thousand rooms upstairs who can say—memory bubbles—every long hallway another corridor into the past.

He wondered whether the sort of article he was outlining might scare away the average tourist, some guy who just wanted to pay his seventeen dollars and get a quiet night's sleep, when a man muttered inarticulately at his shoulder.

"Pardon me," Gander said.

"Gander?" The man spoke so softly Gander barely recognized his own name.

"Mr. Dime?"

"Dime. That's all."

One thin Dime.

The narrow man's pointed face avoided looking directly into

Gander's. With his hat in his hand, he glanced sideways out over the lobby and, when he spoke again, seemed to be speaking to it. "A place to sit down," Dime said, his gesturing hand taking in the entire lobby with a sweep, then poking at a nearby cluster of furniture huddled in the right front corner of the room. He started toward it, and Gander followed to a maroon sofa with high arms and a low cushion, then continued around to a green chair so that he could sit and face him.

"So where's my name in this?" Dime said, sitting down, shiny at the knees, his worn suit blending into the hotel furniture. He sank back deep against the cushion, stretching an arm to either side, the palms of his hands flat on the back of the smooth maroon. His eyes careened off Gander's and wandered across the room, but some center in him was alert, intelligent, there when he glanced into your face.

"Actually, nobody said too much about you. That's why I'm doing the article."

"You said a series. This is a series, you said. You said that to me." His head nodding, his hair thinned and slick on top, his face all angles.

"It is. Hey, no big deal. Just another rescue story. What I want to do is put together . . ."

"Why?"

"Why what?"

"Put together why?"

"No, wait a minute. Go back. The Superlative Man saved some people. It was like a sequence. A guy, you for example, he gets himself in trouble. The Superlative Man's on the other side of town, but he flies over just in time, man saved. The Superlative Man's a hero. Everybody's happy."

"Except with me. Seems everybody wasn't so happy if I remember. And I got a good memory. Take you, for example. I remember you."

"Me?"

"Yeah, you called this morning."

It was a joke. Gander smiled back. Humor him. Lead him around. Catch him looking.

"Might not be here otherwise," Gander bantered. "So anyway, with you it was some disaster in the subway. And when the call came through, the call about you, everything down there was unraveling."

"What call?"

"That you were drifting out to sea. They said you were tied up in a rowboat."

"There was a storm coming."

"You knew that."

"Oh, sure. The water. The water was choppy, very choppy. Terrifying."

"Didn't I read somewhere that you were unconscious?"

"I was. I mean, I knew about it later. It must have been terrifying."

"Whoever called said there was a storm coming."

"Hey, Gander, I never made no call."

"I didn't say that, Dime."

"I was in the boat at the time. Helpless."

Gander wrote in his notepad, heeding Jade's advice: Take your time. Let them do the talking. He eyed Dime. "When the call came through, the Superlative Man was down in the tunnels. They were just starting to flood."

"So?"

"So he has to decide. Can he get back before the subway workers are really in trouble, or does he just let you drift out to sea?"

"Good story."

"I suppose so, but . . . you probably know this already."

"No, tell me. It's real interesting."

"At the time nobody made much of him heading out to save

you, then getting right back. I suppose he figured the water wasn't rising fast enough. He just took off. Nobody counted on a fire."

"Terrible electrical fire." Dime nodded vigorously. "Man almost killed."

"It *was* terrible," Gander said. "His face was burned."

"Doesn't look so good for the Superlative Man, you wouldn't think."

"No, it really doesn't," Gander agreed, his thoughts wandering in spite of himself. "Although I suppose you could say it wasn't really his fault."

"Hey, he's the Superlative Man," Dime asserted.

The conversation lapsed. Gander looked aimlessly about the room, his hands on the armrests, the notepad open in his lap.

"Anyway"—he shook his head, focusing again on Dime and taking a sudden and intense dislike to the man—"I'm not trying to accuse you of anything."

Dime placed a finger on the side of his nose and directed his head several inches to the left. "Why would you do that?"

"I wouldn't. I'm not. I'm saying, I'm not."

"So what's it got to do with the law of gravity?"

A figure of speech.

"Nothing," Gander answered. "It was a lousy coincidence. But there was a string of bad coincidences. So I was wondering, Dime. What d'you think, just bad luck?"

"What's that supposed to mean?"

"Hey, don't get me wrong. I'm not suggesting anything but."

Dime's face relaxed in a grin. "Hey. Of course not."

Gander grinned back. "You don't think I'm hinting around at some evil conspiracy, do you, Dime?"

Dime broke into a hard laugh. "Evil conspiracy!" he exclaimed.

"Hah!" Gander rejoined.

"The Sultan is watching you!" Dime crowed.

Gander's face went flat. "The who?"

Dime looked like he swallowed his tongue. "An expression," he said thickly.

"The Sultan?" Gander repeated gently.

"None of your business."

"Somebody you work for, maybe?" Gander suggested.

Dime retreated. "So the Superlative Man was looking kind of overworked, huh?" he said.

Gander jotted rapidly. "Even the Superlative Man can't be in two places at the same time," he acknowledged, glancing up.

"That's right, he can't, can he?" Dime answered, catching the thread. "Gives you something to think about, right?" His voice rising. "All those headlines? People *dying*, practically. Trains. Floods. Fires. And all the time the Superlative Man's *right there*? I mean, who's runnin' the joint?"

Gander eyed him. "I suppose you could look at it that way."

"Could!" Dime sat up. "Gander, *think*! People don't remember the puny details. Headlines. If you're lucky. And what's the headlines? SUPERLATIVE MAN'S THERE AND THEY ALL CROAK ANYWAY! Kind of infects your thinking, don't you know?"

"Affects. Affects your thinking."

"You bet."

"I don't know, Dime."

"Dime, yeah."

"People still believe in the Superlative Man," Gander observed. "Like it or not, they do."

"They don't know nothin' about him."

"Maybe not, but they believe in him anyway."

"Think about it this way, Gander. What if he starts to look a little like the rest of us? You know. *Not perfect*."

Gander answered, "I know, I know," his thoughts wandering all over again. "The Superlative Man can't save everybody."

"Damn right. And let him slip, you know, a little bit here, a little bit there. Next thing you know, he looks like us. Just another palooka, trying too hard. People get tired. They'll get tired of him, too."

"But what's the point?"

"Hey, what *is* the point. The Superlative Man's a face in the crowd."

"Wait a minute," Gander said, sitting up and setting aside his notepad. "What are we *talking* about? What are *you* talking about? He *saved* you."

"Maybe I dreamed it."

Gander stared across the table. "Hey, Dime. What were you doing in that boat?"

"What's that supposed to mean?"

"Just what it says."

"Whoa. Dangerous talk."

"Then forget I said it. What were you doing in that boat?"

Dime watched him. "You don't hear," he said.

"Maybe you're not getting through."

"Look," said Dime, pointing at Gander's chest, "forget the Superlative Man."

"Maybe I can't forget him. Maybe I think somebody's dragging him down. Maybe I think that's news."

"Oh sure. You'd like him to be the top. Put him in the pilot's seat and climb aboard. You think like a kid."

"I don't know what to think. But I'm starting to wonder. Why don't you tell me what you know about Violet Hayes?"

"Nothin'."

"What's she got to do with the double rescues?"

"Search me."

"Who's running High Water?"

"Haven't a clue."

"Is it the Sultan?"

"You listen to me, Gander. You got nothin' on nobody. If you know what's good for you, you'll keep it that way."

"Is the Sultan out to get the Superlative Man?"

"Forget the Superlative Man. He's as tricky as the rest of us."

"Maybe you're not tricky at all, Dime," Gander answered softly.

"Oh yeah? You got me figured? Well figure this, pal. You dream about the Superlative Man at night? Yah? You think he dreams about you? He dreams about himself."

Dime sat at the edge of his seat.

"Dime," said Gander. "Maybe he dreams about you."

"Like I said," Dime answered, standing, looking down at Gander perched on the green chair, "we all got our dark side." And putting his finger against his nose, and moving his face several inches to the right, he walked away toward the door.

Patty's Desk

Back in the offices of the *Metropolitan Meteor*, Gander stepped from the elevator into the outer lobby of the twelfth floor and walked past the wall of framed front pages. He was thinking about Dime.

Dime and one more interview. One more disaster.

INTERVIEW COLLAPSES!
QUESTIONS IN DUSTY RUBBLE;
ANSWERS LOST

Two interviews now and nothing to show. Not to mention a creeping dread of going at it again. He couldn't even remember where he'd lost the thread. It had started well enough, but after that his mind was a blank. He had no idea whether he'd got within a mile of the important stuff. All he kept seeing was Dime poking his finger into the air and asking what the Superlative Man dreamed about at night. It was as bad as Natasha Nyle. And when he tried to remember *that*, red eyes gleamed at him. Red eyes that changed to big black ones. He was walking through revolving doors and ending up where he'd started. Paul York would have his hide.

He glanced into York's empty office as he passed.

Unless what Jade said was true. Maybe York didn't really want the stories to come off. Hell, he could go in right now. Leave a little note. York, success! I've got *nothing*.

And he thought he'd had the upper hand, smiling at Dime's peculiar humor, leading him on. But who'd been led?

LACKEY NO LOSER,
LICKS LOPER

How had Dime stolen the conversation? How had Gander fallen for it? And what had he fallen into? Again.

As he turned into his office doorway, Patty caught his eye. She was at her desk just inside the door, her hand out palm up. But she was talking into a telephone and Gander waited, watching her, the receiver cradled between her shoulder and cheek, her hands rummaging through the memos, letters, and articles scattered about her desk.

It was only a few weeks earlier, and about two weeks after she was transferred into his office, that Gander had slipped her a note asking if she was free that Friday evening. He'd been eyeing her ever since she arrived. But when he happened by her desk half an hour later, she took the telephone she was speaking into away from her ear, muzzled the receiver against her breast, looked at him squarely, and said, "No." She said it as though she meant it, and the receiver was back to her ear and she was talking before Gander had a chance to respond. Later, back in his cubicle, he confessed to Buddy Lester what he'd done. Buddy delivered a predictable sermon about sex and work being two games that didn't belong in the same arena, but he also told Gander the reason Patty was transferred to Features in the first place. What Gander hadn't known was that he was catching her on a rebound from a thing with Will

Peale, one of the vice presidents in charge of something. It sounded like a boss-chases-secretary-around-the-desk sort of affair, one-sided all the way down the carpet, but whatever it was it ended fast when Mrs. Peale arrived early one afternoon, little Willy Junior in tow.

SECRETARY SLIPS ON
TOP-BANANA PEALE

Her husband's office door was closed but, to his infinite regret, not soundproofed, and they heard Mrs. Peale hollering all the way to Classifieds. Patty was shuffled off to Features the next day.

Peale was known to have a wandering eye, but Gander couldn't fault his taste in this case. Patty was a secretary who could warm your blood if you watched her lick too many envelopes. A brunette with an eye for clothes and a shape to hang them on, she had bright hazel eyes that seemed to see into you and somehow made you look all the harder back at her. Buddy Lester said she used to be an artist's model.

Ostensibly, Gander watched as she sifted through the papers on the face of her desk. Actually, he was daydreaming about the various imaginative poses in which he could paint her in various imaginative states of undress—if he'd been an artist—when he realized that she was staring at him with a peculiar expression.

REPORTER EXPOSED!

"Okay, okay, yeah, I'll call him, okay," Patty said into the phone, raising a single finger to Gander. She would only be a second more. She hung up and her chin dropped to within an inch of the desk. Without lifting her head, she raised her eyes.

"Fifteen minutes," she said.

"Fifteen minutes?"

"Fifteen minutes I've been trying to get off that line!" she exclaimed, sitting up.

"And let me guess. You wanted me to wait for you to get off so you could tell me I should have called in late because you've been trying to reach me for the last hour."

"I've been trying to reach you for the last hour and a half and, yes, you should have called me."

"Patty, I'm sorry."

"You could at least pretend to have some excuse."

He lowered his eyes. "Shy?"

"Shy my foot," she answered and, as though suddenly remembering something, looked in that direction.

"Okay, not shy. Except with women I think about day and night."

"Very funny, mister. Harvey, where have you been? I'm too busy answering your phone calls to get to my work. *Everybody*'s looking for you."

"Yeah? Who's everybody?"

"York, for one. He's only called four times." Patty leafed through a small pile of square white scribbled notes and stopped at the next-to-last one. She looked at Gander. "Natasha Nyle called."

"And you were jealous. Patty."

"Watch it, Gander. Actually, she sounds like a real flake."

"Why? What did she say?"

"Not much really. Just left her number. Out in the borough."

"Okay. Who else?"

"York, York, York," Patty chanted, going through the pile. It sounded like some kind of laugh.

"Did he say what it's about?"

"I dunno," she said. "He mentioned Peale was maybe interested in what you're working on." The moment passed. "He also said something about scrapping your series."

"Scrapping it. Who else?"

"There's no message on this one. He said don't even write it. But you're to call E."

"E?" he said.

"E," she repeated.

Gander leaned over and whispered, "Top see-cret," lingering on the syllables and finishing with a wink. Patty laughed.

"Is that it then?"

"That guy Dime from the list I gave you yesterday."

"When did *he* call?"

"About two minutes before you walked in. He wouldn't leave his number."

"You said you were on the phone."

"I was. Buddy took the message and brought it over."

"And?"

"You want more?"

"It's a chronic condition."

"As a matter of fact there is one more. A woman named Jeannie called. She wouldn't give me her last name. She said you needn't bother returning Natasha Nyle's call." Patty handed him the collection. "All these *women*." She said it with a smile, but she was curious.

Gander answered, "And I'll bet Jeannie didn't sound scared."

"No, not scared. Sort of enthusiastic."

"Patty, I can't stay here. I don't want to see York. Do me a favor? If he calls, you haven't seen me."

"Now wait a minute, Harvey. Other people saw you, and if he starts asking questions . . ."

"Patty."

"What."

"Nobody's going to fire you."

She studied her red polished nails, then looked up. "That wasn't necessary."

"You're right. Sorry. I've been doing this for two days. Everything I say comes out wrong."

"Apology accepted. But watch it, will you? It's hard enough living that down. Everybody thinks they've got the story."

Gander said, "I know the story."

"Oh yeah? And what's the story?"

"Peale's a lech," Gander said. "Always has been. It's a known fact."

"He is. He's a crumb."

"It's a fact."

She smoothed her blouse into her skirt.

"Is everything all right, Harvey?"

"I wish I knew."

"I mean, can I do anything?"

"Yeah, if he asks—when he asks—you can tell York I haven't been in."

"Sure, sure. But can I *do* anything?"

He leaned over her desk, speaking softly. "You could have dinner with me."

Patty glanced behind her into the room. The other reporters were busy on their phones, their voices tumbling together in a soft drone. "Quiet, will you?" she insisted.

He put his finger to his lips, leaned closer to her ear, and said, "Tonight?"

"What time?" she whispered back.

He traced an eight on the surface of her desk. She looked up and nodded. "You'll pick me up?"

He nodded back.

"Wait just a sec," she said.

She jotted her address and number on a blank message pad, and Gander slipped the sheet into his pocket with his other messages.

"Harvey?" she said, her eyes lowered, studying her desk. "Remember when I was on the phone?"

"Yeah, I think so."

She looked up. "You had this *expression* on your face."

"I was thinking about you."

"Liar. I'd give anything to know what you *were* thinking about."

He shrugged his shoulders. "Some other time I'll tell you," he smiled, turning to leave, but he stopped in the doorway and looked back. "Maybe tonight."

Her finger rose quickly to her lips, a slight flick of her eyes indicating the roomful of reporters, now quiet.

Gander galloped twelve flights down a back stairwell to the main lobby of the building, but at the bottom waited, breathing heavily, gently pushing open the door into the lobby just half an inch, scouting for any sign of Paul York. The lobby was deserted and he started across it. He was nearly to the street when a man bending down behind a newsstand counter and reaching into a glass cigar case looked up. Gander stopped, walked back to the newsstand, and lay a dollar on the glass counter.

"Gander!" the man said, straightening right up and placing his hands flat on the glass. His head tilted to one side. A cigar angled at his mouth. "A first!"

"No, Mike, no numbers. Not today. You haven't seen me, and it'd be just like someone I know to check with you."

"Haven't seen you when?"

"Today. This morning. In or out."

"Seen who?"

Gander said, "Owe you one, Mike," turning to go.

"Gander."

He stopped.

Mike pointed at the dollar bill. "Have a little respect, will ya?"

"Mike! What do you think? This is some *bribe*? C'mon. That's for you to play! Any number."

Mike's face broke into a grin and he shot back with conviction, "Name it."

"I don't know. Play the time."

"What time?"

"Whatever time it is when you play it."

Gander stood on the curb edge, surveying the traffic for a break that would let him cross. A taxi rolled by, then a slow bus passed, almost stopped, and roared ponderously on. Gander never even saw her. The taxicab—it sailed right past him. He never even focused on her, there in the backseat. It was only as the dusty bus pulled away in a cloud of fumes and noise that the image of her face resolved in his mind.

"Violet!" he shouted at the street, his voice swallowed whole in the din, the taxi now blocked by the bus and slipping away in the traffic stream. "Violet," he shouted, chasing down the curb, hoping for a red light to halt the suddenly loosening jam. "Violet!" Gander left the curb, one stride into the street, but leaped back at the blast of a horn immediately behind him. A low black coupe with red lines sped past, and he spun around on the sidewalk but it was too late. He doubled over on a parking meter.

The horn of a passing truck tooted, its driver leaning out and jeering. Gander offered him an endearing gesture but limped away down the sidewalk toward the intersection, his hand on his side, his thoughts on Violet: the sickly white skin, the empty black stare. A ghost in a cab.

The Pier

Across the street from the *Metropolitan Meteor*, a twenty-story granite-and-glass tower, sat an architectural cousin, the American Transport building. Inside the American Transport, just beyond the main lobby, a bank of telephone booths lined a long hallway leading back to freight elevators. Across from the first phone booth you had the service exit if you needed to leave in a hurry.

Gander walked along the sidewalk rubbing his bruised ribs, heading up the block from the intersection to the American Transport's main entrance, when the low black coupe with red lines reappeared beside him, slowing at the curb. The passenger door swung open.

"Get in!" the driver invited, leaning across the seat.

It was one of the plainclothesmen who'd been at Gander's apartment the night before. The shorter one. Gander leaned down. "Get out," he said.

"No, get in. It's Violet."

Gander slid onto the seat and slammed the door after him, the car jolting away from the curb. He gripped the armrest. "I don't get it," he said. "You passed me by."

"Didn't see you, y'know, no time to stop. Woulda had a delivery truck humpin' my rear."

"Who *are* you?"

"Me?" The man turned to Gander. "My name's Harvey Gander."

Gander rolled his eyes. "I give up. What's mine?"

"Whatsa matter? Can't remember your own name?"

"It slipped my mind."

A man's voice spoke quietly behind his neck, "It'll come back," and Gander swung fast, cheek first, into the barrel of a gun.

"Eyes front," the voice insisted, and the face of a man emerged in profile past Gander's left shoulder. "I won't use it," he said, "but I won't not use it." It was the other plainclothesman.

"You don't need a gun," Gander said. "I'm not going anywhere."

"Says you," answered the voice.

The car stopped at a traffic light, and the driver turned in his seat to face Gander, as though for a better look.

Gander asked, "Who *are* you guys?"

"We're Harvey Gander," the driver obliged, and he turned back to the road, accelerating under a green light.

Gander answered, "Sounds like somebody I know," watching the passing buildings.

"Settle in for the ride. This won't take long."

"What's this about Violet?"

"Violet who?"

The car continued east, moving toward the river. Gander memorized the driver's face and hands: a little on the short side, at least he looks short sitting down, with a flat red nose and bulbed nostrils—maybe a drinker—green eyes, clipped brown hair, square hat, square face, square, thick fingers. Describe him in two words: Thick. Square.

"Where to?" Gander said.

"Enjoy the ride."

"It always helps if I have something to look forward to. You know, like a destination."

"We'll keep you company," said the backseat partner.

"Get acquainted, so to speak," added the driver.

"Okay. So let's get acquainted. You're Harvey Gander. Who am I?"

"I said *shut up.*" The pistol barrel bounced off Gander's cheek-bone and he crouched forward, his left palm pressed hard against his face.

"What did you go and mark him up for?" the driver griped over his shoulder.

"He wasn't listening," answered the man in the back.

"Well, it was silly," the driver concluded.

Silly. Gander thought about the word. A tiny trickle of blood ran down the back of his hand.

The river gleamed. They drove north into a neighborhood of abandoned piers and slowed beside a wide, flat platform of packed earth stretching deep into the river. The driver swung the wheel, double-bounced over a curb, the broad dirt plane aligning in front of them, and they picked up speed. At the far end of the pier, beyond the fretted line of barrier posts, the shining water sailed fast at them.

Gander shouted above the engine's whine, "If I'd known we were going to commit suicide," his eyes not leaving the water, "I would've left a note."

There are certain silences—far above an engine's roar—where everything seems amplified: the rush in your ears, the light, the sound of the man in the backseat hyperventilating.

The man in the backseat shouted: "Damn it, Karl! SLOW DOWN!"

Karl applied the brake pedal and the car drifted sideways into a long slide. The three men sat in a rising cloud of dust, the river twenty-five feet to their left. Karl turned slowly. For a long time he did nothing but stare into the backseat. When he spoke, his eyes drifting back to Gander, his lips barely moved. "You don't know me, and you don't know my name. You never heard it, you hear? For all you know, it could be Poindexter."

The man in the back snorted quietly. "Poindexter!"

Karl continued. "Wipe the blood off your cheek," he instructed Gander. "And also get out."

Gander reached into his trouser pocket for a handkerchief. He wiped his hand. "Why should I get out?" he said, touching the handkerchief to the wound.

"Just do it."

"Yeah, but why?"

"Look, Gander. If we wanted to shoot you, we would shoot you. Period. No foreplay. We don't wanna shoot you."

"Unless it's necessary," the man in the back qualified.

Karl ignored him. "Now get out, and I'll get out, and we'll both take a little walk alongside the river."

Gander spit into the handkerchief.

"Why would we kill you here?" Karl had apparently found himself in a position worth defending. "Anybody could be watching. Must be ten thousand windows look down on this pier where we are, right now. You still got some, lower down, to the right."

Gander ran the folded edge of the handkerchief along his jawbone. "I see your point," he conceded, studying the stained white cloth. "Karl," he added.

Karl glared into the backseat.

"... but that doesn't explain why you want me to walk over to the river."

"You walk over to the river because my friend in the back here is nervous with his gun."

"And do what?" Gander said.

"Have a little chat."

The gun barrel rising past his ear.

"Right," Gander said, opening the door.

The two men faced each other at the water's edge, Gander locking on Karl's green eyes, resisting a temptation to glance over at the car and the man in the backseat.

Gander asked, "What now?"

Karl answered, "Don't rush me. One thing at a time. I said already, nobody's gonna hurt you. I just thought it would be nice to take a walk and look at the river."

Neither man moved, standing beside the water.

"I always liked this river," Karl confided. "It's just real pretty. And deep as all get out. You could drop something in there," he considered, "and if it was heavy enough, so as it'd go straight to the bottom, you'd never see it no more."

"Or him."

"Yeah, that too," Karl nodded. "Listen, Gander," he said. "You seem okay. I don't know. Maybe you're swell. But I got a little advice for you."

They waited. Gander felt something scramble across his feet and scurry away across the pier, his eyes riveted on Karl's.

Karl said: "You know that story about the curiosity cat? You know what I'm saying? Well, the bottom of that river is home to lots of cats. You might even say it's fe-lined."

A moment passed and he added, "Heh, heh."

The pupils in Karl's green eyes were small and black in the sun. He reached out a hand and laid it on Gander's shoulder. "Okay?" he asked.

But Karl was already starting back to the car. The conversation was over.

"C'mon," he called over his shoulder. "I'll give you a lift back."

. . .

Ten thousand windows, at the very least ten thousand windows, stared flatly back at Gander. It was a beautiful city in the sun. Sparkling stone. Shining white glass. For no conscious reason whatsoever, Gander waved at it all. He waved at the Northern Districts. He waved at Midtown. He waved at the Southern Tier, until his eyes settled on the large white letters on the side of a hulking warehouse far down the river: the American Casket Company, and his arm fell to his side. The Harem. The place Violet told him about. An old casket factory by the river.

Karl's arm reached out from the driver's window, beckoning. Gander walked back to the car, peering into the rear seat as he opened the door and climbed in. The man in the back was slouched down, his chin on his chest, his dark gray hat low over his face.

"You didn't have to kill him on my account, Karl," Gander said, the car crawling down the pier.

The man behind him spoke at his ear. "Shut up and keep your mouth shut."

Karl eyed Gander. "Yeah, and don't say nothing neither." Karl's upper lip pulled back to show his teeth. Karl was smiling. "Hey," he said, the teeth vanishing, "what's the idea wavin' like a yahoo?" He sounded disappointed.

"How should I have waved?"

"Maybe you're seemin' to me like a troublemaker."

"You picked *me* up," Gander shot back, annoyed. "Remember? Wouldn't it have been easier just to send me a threatening letter or something? I mean, why are you guys going to so much trouble just to tell me to shut up and go away?"

"Well, life is just funny, ain't it," Karl answered.

His partner added, "Yeah, maybe that's why it's so short."

"What do you care anyway?" Karl continued thoughtfully. "A little afternoon drive is all."

"Hey, you kidnapped me. And your buddy here about broke my face."

Karl bounced over the curb and into the street, turning south, accelerating. "Yeah, but you wouldn't go to the cops."

"Why not?"

"Would you?"

"No, I suppose I wouldn't."

They turned away from the river back into the city.

Gander said, "Look, I need to talk to you about Violet."

"Is that so?"

"Yeah. I want to know who you guys work for."

"Do you now?"

"Is it the Sultan?"

"You ever get tired of asking questions?" Karl said.

"Put yourself in my shoes."

"Huh," said the man behind him, giving it genuine consideration.

"Out," Karl announced. "Here."

"No, I mean it. Now we need to talk."

"No, *I* mean it. Now you get out."

The gun barrel rising past his ear.

He stood on the curb and watched the low black coupe melt into a wide avenue of traffic crawling west across the city. On the opposite corner a man on top of an upside-down trash barrel was shouting. Wrapped in a purple blanket and wearing a hat that, halolike, had a round brim but no lid, he gesticulated feverishly at passing cars. The man was preaching.

The dead! The dead! They're in your trunks! They hear you. Listen.
Go faster! Faster! Hah! Red light!

The preacher's arms stretched wide to the sunlit windshields. Cars honked. A man leaned out a second-story window, barking unintelligibly. Gander leaned against a light pole and spit into the stains in his handkerchief.

Coffins with steering wheels! Oh, brother, can you spare me a map*! Honk! Honk! I can't* hear *you. Honk your honk. Shine your shine. No such thing as light, no such thing as . . . Honk! The rest is silence. The armrest is silence. Only the light is full of sound! Only the horns shine brightly!*

People were slowing. People were leaning out their apartment windows to listen and call back and forth. Half a block away a cop approached at a brisk clip. Gander turned and slipped through a drugstore doorway.

Past a wall of greeting cards at the rear of the store a red phone booth sat occupied. Inside, a man hunched over, his hat down, his right arm limp at his side. Gander walked over and sat down on a revolving stool at the empty lunch counter, lifted the collection of messages Patty had given him from his jacket pocket, and, propping his elbows on the counter, leafed through them.

"What'll it be?"

A wide man with a brush cut, thick black glasses, and a dirty white uniform stood in front of him, a spatula at his hip.

"Hey, nasty little nick you got there," the man observed. "You wanna buy a bandage? Maybe some disinfectant?"

"Just a cup of coffee."

"No pie?"

Gander stared at him.

"You had lunch? I got specials today."

"Just coffee, bud."

"Mac. The name is Mac."

The phone-booth door opened behind him. Footsteps crossed the tiles to the street door. Mac stood in front of Gander, watching them go.

·   ·   ·

Gander reread the list of four names, sipping black coffee from a white mug.

> L. C. Dime
> Milo Killigrew
> Philippa Fife
> J. E. Meere

He put a small check beside the first name. Three more like that one, he thought, losing a little more ground each time, and maybe I'll achieve total ignorance.

But what choice is there? If I'm going to hide out from Paul York so as not to get canned from the assignment, then I'd better stick to the assignment. York wants me off the story. Karl and his backseat buddy want me off the story, or at least whoever they work for does. So find the story. *Somebody* knows who killed her. Even if the *Metropolitan Meteor* won't print it, some other paper will. Jade has contacts. People are tying weights to the Superlative Man's cape. That's news.

Gander's thoughts rattled along. He couldn't help it.

Early today, a features reporter from the staff of the *Metropolitan Meteor*, a total unknown, was credited with saving the life of the Superlative Man. Locked in a life and-death struggle with vaguely defined forces of evil, the Superlative Man was cornered in some dark place when Harvey Gander, in intrepid pursuit of a story that all around him said could not be done, burst through a foggy barrier in a flash of light and freed the Caped Man. In honor of his debt to Gander's persistence, the Superlative Man granted the reporter an exclusive interview in which he revealed the whole truth. Caught by news reporters following the closed-door session, Gander said that, until today, he had never found what he was looking for, had never known what he was looking for, and on bad days hadn't even known that he was looking. "I only wish my parents could be with me to share this moment," he observed to scribbling reporters.

He left the counter and walked back to the red telephone booth, closed the glass door, and sat down. But he waited, suddenly unable to bring himself to pick up the receiver and dial. His hand lay against his leg, not moving. Something was blocking him, and when he finally recognized it, he flushed with shame. He was afraid to make the next call.

He fumbled with a cigarette, the narrow booth filling with smoke. Mac's voice boomed from behind the counter. "Hey! No smokin' in the booth!"

Gander slid open the door. "Hey, Mac."

"Hey what."

"Make me a turkey sandwich."

"You are a turkey sandwich."

"Lettuce and tomato."

He closed the door, his fingers aligning the edges of the messages in his pocket, his left hand on the cradled receiver, the cigarette jutting from his mouth. Smoke stung his eyes. He pulled the batch of messages from his pocket and set the list of four names on his knee. He dialed the number of Milo Killigrew.

"Yass?" a woman answered.

"Milo there?"

"Ricky? Is that you?" the woman asked.

"Who's this?"

"It's Emily. Milo's not here right now."

"What's up?"

"There's been another overdose downtown."

"Who?"

"I don't know yet."

"Are the papers on it?"

"Oh, it'll be like the others. Only that it was an overdose."

"Because you got to watch those newspaper types. Like that Gander? You heard about him?"

A pause.

"Oh dear," she said quietly, then, speaking away from the receiver, "Simon, it's the reporter who . . ."

The line went dead.

Gander slipped from the booth, signaling to Mac as he walked back to the counter. "How much?" he said.

Mac looked down at the turkey sandwich sitting on the counter. He raised his eyes to meet Gander's. "You can *eat* it first."

"How much?"

"Okay, okay. Let's see. Coffee's ten. Turkey sandwich forty-five. Lettuce and tomato's extra, though," he cautioned, raising the spatula to his shoulder.

Gander dropped a dollar bill next to the plate and walked out onto the sidewalk. Across the street, the sidewalk preacher was still in business on top of the upside-down trash can, oblivious of the two cops standing below him and looking up. The man caught Gander's exit from the drugstore across the street, stared, and pointed directly at him: ". . . so, *you*, look over your shoulder. That *face*! Brother, it will stop you *cold*."

Gander pulled away in long strides. He needed a phone. He shouldn't have left the drugstore so fast. He should have called the next name.

He stepped into a booth at the next corner and dialed his office. "Sports and Features," Patty said.

"Patty, it's Gander. Don't say my name."

"What on earth's going on?" she whispered. "Paul York was down here right after you left. He's furious."

"Forget York. Patty, do something for me. See if you can find

out who bought High Water from Max Water. And something
else, too, but it depends."

"On what?"

"On whether York is around."

"He's not back from lunch yet. He's late."

"Well, make it quick, then. I want you to check his files."

"Are you *kidding*? Harvey, you know what he's like with them."

"It's important."

"What if he *catches* me?"

"Tell him the truth. Tell him I said it was okay."

"Oh, big help. And what should I tell him you're looking for?"

"Clippings on the Superlative Man rescues. Stories about people
he saved."

"But I did that already, Harvey. I checked those stories."

"I know, but I want to know what York's got on these people
in his own files. You know, notes, any letters, pictures. Anything.
And check to see if he's got anything filed under the Sultan."

"The who?"

"Just check it."

"You owe me, Harvey Gander."

"Did anyone hear you say my name?"

"Oh. Sorry. I don't think so. It's pretty noisy in there."

"What time is it?"

"Nearly two-thirty."

"You're kidding."

"No," she said. "It's two-thirty."

"I'll call before five. You're okay on this?"

"Sure, sure. Harvey, is everything all right?"

"I'll call."

He grabbed the handful of messages from his pocket, reading the
telephone number of Philippa Fife as he dialed.

A small, high voice sang timidly on the other end of the line. "Philippa Fife speaking."

"Miss Fife. You don't know me. I want to talk to you."

"Yes, and what did you say your name was?"

"Gander. Harvey Gander."

"Oh yes. I've been expecting you. Any time would be fine."

"You've been expecting me since when?"

"I honestly can't remember. It's been one of those days."

He changed his tone, responding with automatic politeness. "Please don't think me nosy, but may I ask *how* you came to expect me?"

"Yes, well. We'll have a visit. You see, I can't stand talking on the phone with people I've never met. I'll expect you this afternoon?"

"How about in half an hour?"

"It'll do. Have you eaten?"

"Almost."

"As you wish. I'll be having a late lunch."

Gander jotted down her address and apartment number and set the receiver on its hook, then swung open the door and stepped out onto the sidewalk. Down the street the preacher gesticulated to the sky.

Philippa Fife

Somewhere down a hallway of apartment doors a bell chimed three times.

Gander rapped twice on Philippa Fife's door.

A moment passed and the door opened on a small, thin elderly woman. Watery-blue eyes floated behind wire-rimmed glasses. Hands writhed in a short apron.

"Mr. Gander?" Thin, unsmiling lips pursed.

"Miss Fife."

The woman laughed, a short, exhaling note. Her lips pursed more tightly. "I work for her. Come in."

She turned and led him through a dark foyer into an immaculate white sunlit room. Announcing his name, she passed through a white swinging door into a glimpsed white kitchen and was gone.

The white apartment. Everything around him was white. White walls, white molding, white carpet, white chairs, a white tablecloth over the white legs of a dining-room table, white place settings and china for two. Afternoon sunlight streamed through sheer white curtains, bathing the room. Only Philippa Fife's gaudy red dress glowed in living color.

"Miss Fife?"

"Mr. Gander."

He had no idea what he had expected. But if Philippa Fife had been described to him as he drove across the Great Bridge into the Outer Borough to meet her, he would have found it hard to reconcile her description with his conjurings. Far from the frail, antiquated soul he had suspected, she was younger by decades than he'd guessed on hearing her voice, and probably not much older than he. Her face was cherubic, fresh, and full of life, with fine light gray eyes and delicately flushed cheeks, all framed by short waves of auburn hair in a disarray that spoke of deep pillows and casual sheets. Her hair seemed combed by a lover's hands. But her face, not round so much as plump, in the way of her gently swelling lower lip, seemed not to belong to the obesity over which it stared. And it was at the incongruity as much as anything that Gander stared back: her bright red lipstick was nothing but an inadequate hint of the yards of cloth wrapping her featureless corpulence like a spread. She must have weighed 250 pounds, if she ever bothered to weigh herself at all, and he could not have faulted her if she simply chose to forgo the exercise, for he instinctively sympathized with the woman who seemed hidden in the face. As though Philippa Fife were two people, one head and the other body, one trapped high above the massive presence of the other, he longed to rescue her.

"Don't stare at me so, Mr. Gander. It makes me sad."

"I'm sorry," he answered gently. "I didn't mean anything by it."

"I'm sorry, too. You see, I don't go out much anymore. I forget what to expect."

"I couldn't help it," he said. "Your face is so beautiful."

"Yes, my face. That is still mine. Sit down, please. At the table."

She shoved her body forward to the edge of her chair and stood, slowly but without difficulty, rising to balance her huge frame on tiny red sandals. Stepping toward the dining room table with slow

grace, and indicating to Gander that he should take the white captain's chair at the table's head, she allowed him to hold out her
own chair as she lowered herself onto it. He forewent any attempt
to slide it further under the table, and she inched it forward without sound as he sat down, the sheer white curtains bright behind
him.

Gander had resolved during his drive out to her home to do
none of the talking, or as little as possible. She should talk. And
he would let her, listening. But he found now that he had nothing
to say. Clear thoughts refused to resolve, but filtered away in the
strange emotions overtaking him.

"My face," she said again. "Still mine." Her high tiny voice
fluttering homeless, absurd, a birdsong on an ocean wave. "My
body I gave away, day by day, until there was nothing left to give.
It's the way these things go, you know. Tiny temptations. A little
at a time. For me it was narcotics. I wasted away."

"Narcotics."

"Narcotics. And in the end I was retired with a golden appetite
and an apartment where I could satisfy it in solitude. It took me
all of a year to escape that hunger, another to balloon into this.
Do you understand? I had to substitute *something*. I ate like a sav-
age. Now that, too, is over. Although something happened, some
chemical change. I'll never be able to lose this weight. Believe me,
I've tried. Until it turned into a search for my old lost self, I tried."

"Narcotics," Gander echoed.

"A narcotic," she answered. "I loved it. I chased it like a lover.
All I ever wanted was to be ravished. But I was young then, and
from a distance life looked so romantic. Though life never ro-
manced me. I was merely in demand. But you make no mistake. I
loved the men who came my way: no false motions, no feigned
emotions. I *loved* them, heart and soul and body. I gathered them
in, the full harvest of my embraces."

Even as she spoke, an unreal silence settled over the room, and Gander felt drawn to it as though expecting something, suddenly, in all that whiteness, to darken and move.

"And now," she laughed, a high short flight, "now I look back and for the life of me I can only see naked men thrusting into a naked woman, flat on her back and out of her mind, a drug addict, a whore. Ah, youth."

She smiled, and for a moment revealed the face of a wearied lover, the shy after-love, the silent conspiracy of pleasure following complicity in outrageous abandon; a smile made vague in the knowledge of what it means to be vulnerable. As though her sexual energies had somehow rechanneled into her bold talk, and the dining-room table had become her bed. Though Gander was complicit only in his silence, which he guarded, and the measured smile painted on his face.

"You see, Mr. Gander, *I* now see. I have no more illusions. Or regrets. The patterns of my life are in stone. Stare at them too long and one day you'll look up to find yourself in a museum. No. I believe in what *will* be, because in what will be lies also what *might* be, and there hang the constellations of my day. And one day someone will walk through that front door, like you walked through that door. Perhaps it will be a day like today. Perhaps it is today. Maybe it's you."

Gander held her gaze. Neither moved. Her light gray eyes glistened like something Arctic.

"It isn't you, of course. I'm not disappointed. I knew the moment I saw you. Don't go thinking I rattled on because it *was* you. But I suppose I'm making you uneasy."

She waited. Gander shook his head.

She resumed. "I am philosophical about my weight, in case you hadn't noticed. There was an artist I knew, a boy, and I was a girl. He sculpted stone, and he would search and search for the right piece, picking up thousands. Thousands. Then he would pick up one and recognize it, and he would carry it back to his studio. And with no design, no plan, nothing to tempt him, he would begin to cut. Bit by bit the shape emerged, a shape that had waited from the beginning of time. Waiting just like me. He set it free."

Her eyes dropped to a tiny white china bell and she lifted it in the painted ends of her hand. The maid approached as the frail ringing died away and stood at Philippa Fife's side, the white kitchen door swinging closed behind.

"Will you be eating?" asked Philippa Fife.

He nodded.

The meal was spare and suited to the room: cold potato soup, chicken salad in a shell of cold lettuce, chilled white wine. They ate in silence, and Gander sipped his wine, wondering, What if she had nothing more to say? What if she asked him suddenly to leave? As the meal drew to a close, he directed his attentions toward forestalling that event.

"Miss Fife."

"Philippa, please."

"And you can call me Harvey."

"As you wish," she allowed, speaking as though the name he tendered were an arbitrary thing, as though he could just as easily have said, "Call me Wally" or "Call me Bob." Something had changed as she ate, metabolically. Not only was her earlier enthusiasm for self-revelation now suspect, but Gander saw that there was a better than even chance she would now lapse into her other self: dull, monosyllabic fatness.

"I thought I'd wait until we finished eating," he ventured, "but I was hoping to steer the conversation around to what happened a couple of months ago." The silence in the room deepened, as though he had put his foot through a Chinese paper screen.

"Yes, yes, the Superlative Man. The wonderful Superlative Man."

"I expect you recall the events of that day vividly," he continued, taking his pen from his inner jacket pocket and only at that moment realizing his notepad lay on the front seat of his car, a block and a half away.

"No," she sighed. "In fact, I can't remember a thing."

"*Nothing?*"

"I was high as the wind."

"But you said you stopped. You said you stopped using drugs."

"Yes, well. Let's just say that for one day someone thought it might be fun for me to go out once more, for old time's sake. The hours of that day ran like watercolors. I could no more tell you what happened than I could go back in time and relive it."

"But you must remember *something*," he insisted, "and when you heard the story later, it must have brought *some* of it back." And then, more quietly: "Any of it?" He veered suddenly away, reciting what little he knew: "You were tied to the railroad tracks. On a mountain curve. The conductor would never have been able to . . ."

"*Enough!*" she cried.

Gander stared back at her, deeply disappointed. The more he pressed on, the further some part of him seemed to drift backward. All around questions lay unanswered, as the murders and messages crowded in. He felt as if he were on a train, accelerating into empty spaces. Herds of buffalo thundered along beside his car, but slowed as the train sped faster. For a magical moment they seemed to hover, hanging in a balance, suspended. When something shifted and, slipping away, they galloped backward into the darkness.

She continued, composing her thoughts one by one and dropping them like bad chords. "You describe that rescue as if it were some cartoon."

"But can't you see that's what I'm trying to get *away* from?"

"I can be of no help. That day is beyond recall. Don't be too hard on yourself, though. None of this is your doing."

"No," Gander refused. "It's not good enough. The whole story about you tied to railroad tracks, it's too silly. It's too *much* like a cartoon. Things like that just don't happen in real life, not by themselves. What were you *doing* out there, Philippa?"

"That's enough," she asserted. "You may leave."

"*Leave?* But why did you *invite* me here?"

"Don't be simple. Surely you guessed the answer to that."

"I couldn't begin," he frowned.

"Don't you toy with me," she answered sharply. "If you want to talk, then we should talk. You came on like gangbusters, going out to interview Natasha Nyle, urging her to talk."

"She didn't tell me anything!" Gander reacted, but drew up short. "What could she tell me?"

"And the night before, showing up at High Water. Now that's interesting."

"What's that supposed to mean?"

"I'm warning you. Don't play games."

"Stuff it, Philippa. What about High Water?"

"I'll ignore that remark," she said to her empty plate. "No, I don't believe in coincidence, Harvey Gander."

You and everyone else, he thought.

"Listen, Philippa. It was pouring rain. I was in that part of town and I used to know High Water. I did *not* know it had changed hands. It used to be just a hangout for reporters."

"And actresses."

"And some actors and actresses," Gander admitted, his face reddening.

"Including one particular actress," Philippa answered, her eyes small and black.

"I hadn't seen her in months. How would I know she'd be there?"

"Perhaps you didn't. But if you were to go looking for her, it would be the logical place to start."

"If, if," Gander resisted.

"Oh, but you *did* go there, and you *did* talk to her. And it was only the very next day that someone *did* kill her."

"*Me?* So *I* killed her? *That's* funny."

"It's hardly a joke. I also hear you were there when they found her body."

"It *was* a coincidence."

"Of all the places in this very large city."

"It wasn't me," Gander denied, the words sounding trite and useless, even to him.

"You were, am I right, her spurned lover?"

"No, no, no. Months ago. Longer."

"And am I right that you and Violet exchanged words at High Water the other night?"

Gander was silent.

Philippa said, "I hear that after your little tiff with Violet you got very, very drunk. Think about it, Harvey. Think about all the things each one of us, in our own way, can set in motion."

He stared at her, thinking, This is what it will be like. They'll arrest me, and over and over again this is what it will be.

"Oh, but of course," she taunted. "You've seen nothing, heard nothing. The proverbial monkeys have found a home on your back. Soon you may remember nothing."

"If that's a veiled threat . . ."

"I am not in a position to threaten you. I am no longer in a position to do much of anything, in case you hadn't noticed. If I was, and wanted to, I would not beat around the bush. You would know it."

"Well, you're just wrong."

"I'm supposed to believe that for one moment you didn't hope to find Violet at High Water?"

"Hope and expect are two different things," he answered.

"So you admit you wanted to find her there. You see, I know these things. It isn't necessary to . . ."

Gander interrupted: "I hadn't seen Violet in months."

"No, but you went looking for her at High Water, and a few

hours later she turns up on the floor of some merry-go-round? People are even saying she planned to meet you there."

"No."

"That maybe she even sent you a letter asking you to meet her there."

Gander asked quietly, "Who told you that?"

"And it all makes so much sense. No, I do not believe in coincidence. But I do believe that you are looking like a hanged man."

He slouched in his chair, staring at the table.

"And you'll get what you deserve," she declared, "barging in on something you don't understand, making a bigger mess of it than it already was."

"It was a story. Just a story."

"It is *not* just a story. It's about real people, Harvey Gander. We *need* someone. Someone who can take us back to the way it was before. Before High Water, before the Sultan, before Karl. Someone who can save us from these men."

"Then *start* me somewhere. Philippa, at *least* do that. Tell me who the Sultan is."

"Everything, but everything, is in balance," she babbled.

"Excuse me?"

"All life has its counterlife."

"What counterlife?"

"The Sultan is the evil one."

"Philippa, what are you talking about? Who is the Sultan? Does *he* own High Water?"

"Those *men*," she wailed. "Those *business* men. They're evil."

"Karl? What does he want?"

"They want to control him."

"Who! Damn it, who!"

The fingertips of her right hand drifted down her cheek, a knuckle bending at her lips. Her voice softened. "I know you're anxious, but I'm afraid . . ."

"What do they want with *me*? What do these people *think*?"

But Philippa continued, suddenly disconnected, talking to herself, "... and you're probably not sleeping well, waking from nightmares and looking over your shoulder, not a clue what you're up against, which of course only makes whatever it is loom that much larger ..."

"What do you *believe* in, Philippa?" Gander demanded. And then he was standing, shouting at her, his hands on the table edge, his face leaning down into hers: "*I said, What do you believe in, Philippa!*" But he dropped back against his seat, slapping his palm against the table.

It wasn't sobbing. Philippa's fine gray eyes welled and two pulsing tracks coursed down her face, but the tears formed and died in silence. "You have to go," she said quietly. "Even the walls listen." She glanced across her shoulder to the swinging door where the tiny maid now leaned against the white wall, one hand writhing in her apron, the other holding a glass of clear liquid. Philippa Fife smiled at Harvey Gander as the maid appeared at her side, dabbing the wet with a white handkerchief, lifting the glass of clear liquid to her lips to drink. Philippa drank deeply. The maid looked across the table. "It's time for you to go," she said.

Philippa interrupted: "Don't ask me why I cried. That's one question I could never answer."

She drank again, this time greedily.

"I didn't just mean ..." Gander began but broke off.

"I know what you meant," Philippa assured him. "And I don't know how to answer you. He tells us to believe in balance. Everything, but everything, is in balance."

"He," Gander repeated.

"And it's true, when you think of it. This notion of balance. It grows on you." She smiled vaguely, drowsily, and Gander realized he was losing her.

"*Who* says this?"

"My friend, my keeper, my superlative man."

"*The Superlative Man?*"

"No. *My* superlative man." But the words fell without emphasis, as though she were weary, suddenly spent.

Gander pressed, even as she slipped away. "Philippa, tell me who the Sultan is."

"All life has its counterlife," she answered. But the words were meaningless, a lifeless repetition. Her eyes sagged heavily.

"Who *is* he?" Gander pursued.

"The Sultan is the evil one." She leaned forward onto the table, her head on her arm, her eyes drifting to a close.

"Why can't you be *free*?" Gander whispered.

"Ha!" she exclaimed, her eyes shutting, her mouth sagging against the tablecloth, her face ugly.

Gander looked up. The maid was gone. He left his chair and moved quickly to the swinging door, but the maid opened it even as he reached out his hand.

"You have to go," she said.

"What was she going to tell me?"

The maid stepped out and let the door swing closed behind her. "Miss Fife loves to talk," she said, "but she gets so few visitors. As you see, she *is* hard to follow at times."

Gander stared at her fish eyes, but turned back to Philippa Fife, flopped against the table like a beached whale. He placed two fingers against her neck. A slow steady pulse marked time.

"She's asleep," he said. But when he turned again, the maid was gone, and he stopped flat at the locked swinging door.

In the wide white apartment, he was alone.

When he reached the last flight of stairs, he was skipping three at a time.

He hit the street running.

Bar Bar

As he drove up the bridge to its wide crest, high over the river, his scattered thoughts gathered into a single pressing need to find out who killed Violet. People saw them together at High Water. They knew about the letter. He was there when they found her. It was only a matter of time before the police came looking.

Something darkened and moved to his left. He glanced out the window at a low black coupe with red lines and a squared hood, racing beside him. The front passenger window framed a man in a side-angling hat, his lips spread flat in a smile. Karl's partner. The backseat gunner. The police impersonator. Gander stole a glance at the road ahead. He looked back. A black pistol sat on the door rim, aimed at his face. The moment condensed into the hollow point. But the black car fell away, slipped across Gander's rearview mirror, and pulled up fast on his right. Karl sat at the wheel. Karl turned his thick square face to Gander. Karl was not smiling.

At the far end of the bridge most of the toll booths sat empty, barred by black-and-white striped crossing gates. Only two booths on the far right were open, and a long line of cars sat at each, waiting to pay and pass through. The lane on the left was slightly longer and Gander steered into it and came to a stop, waiting for the black coupe to pull up beside him on his right. It did, idling at his side. Karl eyed him with distaste and turned back to his windshield. The seconds passed. When at last another car pulled to a stop behind the black coupe, Gander swung his wheel hard to the left, kicking the accelerator to the floor, speeding sideways across the plaza. Beyond the tollbooths a policeman bolted from a surveillance hut. Gander swung hard right, closed his eyes, and sailed through a black-and-white crossbar, his foot hard to the floor. It snapped like a match stick and he shot into an open plaza on the other side, aiming at a down ramp into the town's north end. He glanced in his rearview mirror just before the plunge. The black car was behind him, accelerating away from the toll booth with the broken gate, a motorcycle cop racing at it sidelong. Gander missed the interception. His car was careening down a curving ramp at seventy-five miles an hour.

He slowed at the first sight of other cars, braking to thirty-five near a stop sign at the bottom and shooting through a gap in traffic to an immediate chorus of horns. He cut down a cobbled side street, lurching and weaving out of the path of oncoming cars, and made it to the West Side without stopping, slowing just long enough at each intersection to spot a police cruiser or a traffic cop before continuing west on back streets. At Battle Avenue he cut north and a few blocks later turned into a dead-end delivery alley, where he abandoned his car.

Five long minutes on an underground platform, a blue uniform with a silver badge fifteen feet behind him. A garbled announcement said something about a train and went on to catalog twenty stops on the line, but the train roared into the station before the announcer was halfway home and the noise swallowed his voice whole. The train squealed to a stop. Gander stared at a pair of closed doors and the dark interior of an empty car. All up and down the line, lights were on and doors stood open, people pouring in and out. He sprinted to the nearest open car, slipping through as the doors closed behind him and they pulled away, the world outside going black as the train shot into the tunnel. He sidled through passengers to an empty spot at the far end of the car, where he stood by the door that led through to the next car, the dark and empty one. A flash of electricity burst outside the train. Ceiling lights flickered and died, paralyzing riders in night-blue freeze frame. A moment of absolute black gave way to gradual flickering, then a full white bath as the ceiling lights regained power.

Gander turned to his reflection in the glass, the empty car beyond it a dark background. From deep within the empty car a burst of blue flame shot toward him, transforming even as it exploded, apparitionlike, into the streaming hair and dead white skin of Violet Hayes, her arms outstretched, her face screaming into the roar.

Blackout. Flickering gold. White bath.

His face in the window watched his face in the window.

He shoved his way out of the train at the Harrison Street Station, glancing back over his shoulder. The doors of the empty car stood wide, white lights blazing. He moved in long strides to an escalator and rose from the station into the gilded lobby of the Eternal Life Insurance building. Beyond a newsstand a bank of telephones clung to a wall. He passed them by, turning down a dingy side hall toward a lone telephone booth opposite service elevators. He slid the door closed behind him, unscrewed the ceiling light, and sat in the shadows.

Where to start? He tried Violet's old number. The line rang nine times, his face pressed against the greasy receiver.

Smoke drifted from a cigarette across the cradled receiver. A friendly woman rapped at the glass. If he wasn't using the telephone? Gander ignored her, picked up the phone, and rang the operator.

"High Water," he said. "Stage Alley."

He relayed the number to the inside of a matchbook and dropped in another nickel.

"High Water," a voice answered and Gander almost said, "Steve," but caught himself. "Billy Bolder there?" he asked.

"Who wants to know?"

"Johnny Harrison. Musical Artists."

"He's got a job."

"Who are you? His mother?"

"Wait a second."

A minute passed. Something on the floor was burning. The booth was clouded with smoke.

Billy growled. "Bolder. Who's callin'?"

"Don't say my name. It's Gander, Billy. Call me Johnny Harrison. I'm an agent."

"What can I do for you, Mr. Harrison?"

"I have to find out about Violet, Billy."

"Yeah, well, I know some guys who might work. Problem is finding them, you know. Could be anywhere."

"Yeah, but you could tell me where to start."

"I'm not so sure, mister. Maybe they're interested in talking to you, maybe they're not."

"On the level, Billy. I'm in trouble. I need your help. I'm at the Harrison Street Station. Can you meet me here?"

"Sure, Gander. I'll be right over." And the line went dead.

Gander sat in the booth without moving, the minutes passing, then stared wide-eyed at the receiver. He slammed open the folding telephone booth door and charged away down the hall to the freight entrance.

• • •

He waited on the curb for cars to clear, a low black coupe with red lines and a squared hood appearing at the far corner. But Gander never saw it as he cut across the street and ducked down a short stairwell into a Chinese restaurant.

The place was smoky and crowded with voices and clattering plates. Down a little hallway past a hat-check girl he found a pay phone and stuck the receiver between his shoulder and his face, the list of four names in his hand.

> L. C. Dime
> Milo Killigrew
> Philippa Fife
> J. E. Meere

They all know each other. Satellites breed all around them. Somebody wants me, but who? The Sultan? Who *is* this guy, and why's he after *me*? They're fishing. They could have had me by now. They want me, and they want to watch me run.

And then it clicked. J. E. Meere. Jeannie. Gander dropped a nickel in the box and dialed.

"Hello?" she answered.

"Hello, Jeannie. It's Harvey Gander."

"Harvey. We were just talking about you."

"I need to see you, Jeannie," he said.

"Harvey, Harvey, Harvey," she chanted. "What are we going to do with you?"

"I was hoping you had that figured out. You know, save me the trouble?"

"What's the matter? Tired of the newspaper business?"

"Jeannie, I don't want to interview you. I just want to talk to you as a friend of Violet."

"Harvey, I like you. But now? Right now? No can do, my friend."

"Do me this, Jeannie."

"You want a favor?" she said. "Okay. From the heart. Some friendly advice. You should go away. You know, from High Water, from Violet. Really. Go back to wherever you came from. So long, Harvey."

She hung up.

Gander replaced the receiver, watching the phone as though hoping it would ring. Someone was approaching down the little hallway, and his eyes followed. Karl and his partner blocked the way back into the restaurant.

Gander turned to meet them. "Can I help you fellows?"

"Oh, thank you, no," answered Karl's partner. "We were just waiting to use the telephone."

"Well then, I guess I'll be getting back to my table. Wouldn't want to keep the little lady waiting."

Karl said, "Just a minute, Gander."

"Gander? Gander?" answered Gander. "There must be some mistake. The name, my friend, is Wallace. William Wallace. Now, if you'll excuse me." He moved sideways to step between them, but they closed ranks. "Now wait just a minute here," Gander cautioned, taking a step back. He pointed a finger into the air, looked meaningfully at them, and, as loud as he could, screamed, "*FIRE!*" A woman in the restaurant shrieked. Waiters came running, and Karl and his partner swung around to intercept them, Karl sticking his palms out like a traffic cop. Gander exploded between their shoulders, erupting into the restaurant and shouting, "*Out front! Everybody out front!*" as he dodged among people and tables, angling back to the kitchen, the restaurant surging away behind him toward the front door. And he was through the narrow kitchen and sprinting down an alley to the next street, two blocks away in the backseat of a cab, hyperventilating and sweating into his shirt, before he finally looked back.

The driver aimed east, Gander watching the traffic through the rear window. No one followed. He said, "Here," and the cabbie pulled up at the curb, a telephone booth rising beside them.

Inside the booth, he dialed the *Metropolitan Meteor*.

"Elmo Jade," he said, and the telephone clicked through the transfer and rang.

Standing in the glass booth beside the street, he was hugely visible, a gallery exhibit, cars lined up and passing by to stare inside.

A woman's voice answered. "Mr. Jade's office."

"He there?"

"He's out right now. Any message?"

"Where can I reach him?"

"Who's calling?"

"A friend."

Jade's voice in the background whispering, "Who is it?"

The line went silent.

Then, "Jade here."

"It's Gander."

"Nice timing."

"What's happening?"

"You are, my friend."

"I don't know what's going on, Jade. I only know all of a sudden they're chasing me."

"You found out something, didn't you?"

Gander paused, his back to the passing cars, his eyes down. "No, nothing. Tell me what you know."

"I hear you and Violet were an item, Gander."

"Who told you?"

"It changes things. She ran with a fast crowd. When did you two go out?"

"A while ago. A long time ago."

"The word is you came around after her."

"There's something I should've told you, Jade. Where we found her at the carousel, I was supposed to meet her there. I got a letter from her the same time I got that little stone man. But when she took off in a car headed the other way, I didn't know what to do. That's when I called you. I just didn't know what was happening. Jade, I'm scared."

Jade was quiet for what seemed like a long time. "You're right," he said finally. "You should've told me."

"I didn't want anyone to think I killed her."

"You can't control what people think."

"It wasn't me," Gander answered. "I swear it wasn't me. But they're trying to pin it on me. And they know about the letter."

"They know you went out with her?"

"Yeah."

"Did you love her?"

Gander said, "I was crazy about her."

"What about her? Did she love you?"

"You know. We fell in love and she went away."

"C'mon. Don't be such a tough guy. Talk to me."

"I didn't know she was mixed up in this, Jade."

"But now you think she might have been."

"What do *you* think?"

"Me? I'm guessing. I think it's you they don't know what to do with."

"They *who*?"

"Whoever killed her."

"Jade, what are the cops saying? Do they think I did it?"

"Not yet. Mostly the talk is still about her. I don't think anyone knew where she came from."

"Some little town," Gander answered. "She ran away from home, she ran away from her parents, she ran away from me. When I saw her at High Water, she was still running."

"From what?"

Gander answered, "Getting too close," his voice dropping.

"Meaning you don't want to talk about it."

"No, meaning getting too close to somebody. She gets close, and she bolts. Oh man, look, I'll call you later."

"*Whoa!* Do *not* hang up."

But Gander cradled the receiver.

Talking about her like that brought too much of it back. It was like when he saw Frankie Bullock in that uptown diner. You spend the whole time trying not to remember the conversation that circled round and round, and then: "I'm sorry, Harvey. I'm just sorry." Violet standing by the door. Later in his apartment, sitting there by himself, he cried for the first time since he was a boy, his face wet like it was melting.

In a phone booth by the curb, Harvey Gander watched the low, dark animals pass slowly by.

He backed out onto the crowded sidewalk, shapes to weave through, people shifting, a dreamlike maze. On a wall beyond the passersby an amber word pulsed and glowed: BAR BAR.

Inside, the room rolled back into shadows like a railroad car, the long bar trailing away on the left and drifting into a final hard curve. A few men sat scattered down its length, their drinking glasses stationed before them on the polished wood, their heads down.

Gander took an empty barstool close to the door, his hands flat on the wood, studying the faces of the drinking men. He shouted at them, his voice filling the empty room: "It's all about *love*, that's what it's all about." But his voice broke off, a donkey bray, and he sank down above his stool, his shoulders sloping, his elbows leaning into the bar.

A bartender appeared before him. "You say something?" he asked, his left brow raised.

Gander looked up. "So maybe I did," he answered, his body inflating. "I said maybe I'm gonna get drunk." The bartender waited, his short white towel hugging his shoulder. Gander looked straight into the bartender's clear eyes. "I came in here to get drunk," he elaborated.

"So what'll it be?" The bartender glanced with a flick of an eye at his wristwatch, looked down the picket line of patrons, and turned back to Gander.

"But now that I'm here," Gander answered, thinking out loud, his eyes now locked on the bartender's, neither man blinking, "I think maybe I'm changing my mind."

The bartender leaned down into his heels, shoved his fists into his pockets, and nodded slowly, his oiled black hair shaking and shimmering in the bar light. "You know," he said, "I could go along with you, or I could walk down the bar, refill their glasses, and go back to my paper."

"Look at those guys," Gander suggested.

"What about 'em?"

"They don't even know the difference," Gander said.

"And you do?"

"Yeah, maybe I do. The difference is that maybe I'm changing my mind."

"You're not going to get drunk."

"No, I think maybe I'm not. Don't get me wrong. I'd like to get drunk. I'd like to get beautifully drunk. But you know, that's not going to make it go away."

"If you get drunk," said the next man down the bar. The man was sitting up and watching Gander. All down the bar, men had lifted their faces from their speaking tubes. They were watching Gander, their white faces and wet eyes wavering like a line of reeds.

"If I get drunk," Gander agreed. "But I'm not going to, because I think I changed my mind."

The barkeep nodded, and on down the length of the room the bodies bobbed in recognition that something had happened, or that perhaps the day was passing, or that the man at the far end of the bar, the man down there with the bartender, was talking.

"Because I have to find out what happened to her," Gander said.

"And therefore," said the barkeeper, "you will not get drunk."

"I just changed my mind."

"You did," the bartender agreed. "I saw it."

From the doorway Gander looked back, nodding to the barkeep, nodding generally to the men posted down the length of the bar, the men nodding and wavering as in a breeze.

In the telephone booth on the curb, Gander dialed High Water.

"High Water," the answer. It was Steve.

"Steve. It's Harvey Gander. Let me talk to Billy Bolder."

"Hey, Gander, I don't know."

"Put him on."

"Just wait."

Gander glanced at his watch. Seven-twenty. The place should be packed, but the line was quiet.

"Bolder here."

"It's Gander, Billy."

"So I hear."

"Tell them they can pick me up on Redgate. Near the corner of Bath. I'll be waiting."

Bolder paused. "I don't know, wha'd'ya mean? Waiting for who?"

"Karl and his buddy. The two guys you told about me being at Harrison Street."

Gander hung up and swung open the sliding door. He stepped out onto the sidewalk, planted his fists on his hips, and locked his eyes on the edge of the roof far above the entrance into the bar.

"Yes," he whispered.

Milo Killigrew

He was waiting on the corner when the low black coupe with red lines slowed to a stop at the curb. Karl looked out the window. He was alone. "Get in, Gander," he said.

Gander greeted him: "Hello, Karl," and opened the passenger door and slid in, pulling it closed as the car slipped away from the curb.

"Where to?" Gander asked.

"Rest easy. We'll get there."

"Just curious."

"Just shut up."

The car sat in front of High Water, Karl holding open Gander's door. Gander stepped out onto the sidewalk, and Karl gripped his upper arm and steered him through the outside entrance. Halfway down the unlit stairway to the bottom door, Gander felt a hand flatten in the middle of his back. He landed in the stairwell on his hands and knees, the door pulling open in front of him. Somewhere above a pair of shoes and trouser cuffs, a voice was speaking.

"Milo," Karl said regretfully. "He slipped and fell."

"These stairs," Milo agreed.

Karl answered, "Yeah, you can't see nothing."

Footsteps plodded away up to the street. Gander stood with care.

"He should not have done that," said Milo.

Milo. Milo Killigrew. The man with the gun. The second name on the list. Karl's partner.

He stood five-ten, maybe a shade under six feet, his eyes sunken and his skin pasty in the low light, his thick black hair greased to a low sheen. "Why don't you come in," he offered and stood aside, holding open the door. Gander walked through but stopped when he heard a key turn in the lock behind him.

High Water was empty and leaden, lit only by a handful of miniature white lights along the border of the mirror behind the bar and, across the room, a doorway framing a soft rectangle of gold light. Milo passed Gander by, Gander watching him move through the shadows until he turned, a silhouette in the doorway.

"Listen, Gander," he said, his voice carrying easily. "You don't need to think about it. Come along with me. There's somebody waitin' for you."

Gander followed him into the back hallway, under the glow of a single overhead bulb, past doors marked Ladies and Gents and ending in one last door, marked Private. Milo unlocked it and they passed through into a second hall lit by a single overhead bulb, passed a glass office door, and kept walking until the hallway ended flat in one last door. A sign on it read, Janitor. Milo gestured at it.

"It's a janitor's closet," Gander said.

Milo stuck his hand in his trouser pocket and lifted out a small ring of keys. He held them out to Gander. "I know," he said. "Open it."

"Wait a minute, Milo. I'm not so sure about this."

"Look, Gander, everything's gonna be okay. We got a little somethin' for you. Now open the door," he instructed, holding out the key ring, a single key extended.

Gander unlocked it. A light burned inside.

"It is a janitor's closet," he said.

"Yeah. Get in."

"You're locking me in a janitor's closet?"

"No. I'm comin' with you. Now get in."

"No."

"Look, Gander," said Milo, a slight edge now, his hand reaching beneath his jacket. "I told you, you got nothin' to worry about." When his hand reappeared, a snubnosed revolver pointed at Gander's chest. "So *okay*?"

"Sure, Milo, sure. It's okay, it's okay."

The two men stood close together inside the closet, their shoulders touching, Milo pulling the door closed.

"You can put the gun away," Gander suggested.

"Just open the fuse box behind you. Above the sink. With the little silver key."

Gander reached back across his left shoulder and unlocked the gray box.

"Now press the third fuse down, on the left. Keep it down and push in the fourth fuse, the one in the middle."

"These?"

"Yeah. Push 'em."

A mechanism clicked beneath the floor and the room began to drop.

"You're kidding," Gander said.

But Milo only grinned at him and they descended in silence, until a new door rose from the floor in front of them, and the closet stopped. Milo turned the knob. Another hallway stretched away. He gestured at Gander with the gun as though it were his hand. "C'mon," he said, "it's this way."

They walked side by side to the far end of the hall, where they stopped and faced two doors.

"Go ahead and open the one on the left."

Gander waited. He looked back over his shoulder to the door to the elevator.

"Oh, come on, will you?" Milo said and pushed through. Gander followed him into a room tiled in black and white squares, like a chess board. A floor-to-ceiling mirror covered the wall to the right, and a floor-to-ceiling mirror covered the wall to the left. Between the mirrors, stretched across the wall opposite the door they'd entered, hung a deep red curtain.

The two men faced one another, their repeating reflections spreading away into the distance in long curves.

"There's no one here," Gander said.

"We'll get to that," said Milo, nodding at Gander, his hands on his hips, the gun pointing sideways at the mirror. "But you're seemin' to me a little nervous."

"Hey, Milo. You brought me down here with a gun."

"Hey, nobody's gonna hurt you. You know that. Look at you, comin' over here and all."

"I came over here because I need to find out about Violet."

"Look, forget about Violet for two seconds, okay? I want to talk to you. See, we were feelin' bad about the way we were treatin' you. So we thought we'd make it up." Milo started away toward the edge of the red curtain. "I told you. Everything's gonna be okay now," he explained, " 'cause we got a little somethin' from us to you." One hand slipped behind the curtain folds, the gun hanging at his side, his arm reaching up and down behind the red cloth, the heavy drapery parting to reveal Natasha Nyle. In a soft red light. Sitting stretched on a bed and facing them. She was almost naked in a white bra and short slip, her ankles bound together with white rope, her arms tight behind her. A stretch of white tape sealed her mouth. A narrow white blindfold wrapped her face.

Milo started back toward Gander. "She's yours, Gander. All night long." He nudged Gander in the ribs with the point of the gun. "I'm heading back upstairs. Don't do nothin' I wouldn't do."

A long silence.

Then, "You're kidding me."

The grin evaporated. "Meaning what?"

"Just what I said," Gander answered. "You're kidding me." Shaking his head, staring at Milo.

"Maybe Karl was right," Milo said evenly. "Maybe you are a troublemaker."

"What the hell do you think I'm *doing* here?"

"Why *did* you come here, Gander?"

"I want to know what happened to *Violet*."

"Is that so?"

"Yeah, it is."

"Well, now you're here, pal. And I'm tryin' to be a nice guy. And we go and shut the place down just for you."

Something was changing in Milo's eyes. They were smaller, darker. "But I think you're gettin' to be a pain in the ass, Gander. And I think maybe you should start mindin' your own business."

Gander sensed something to the right and looked that way. It was his reflection in the mirror.

"All I want to do is find out what happened to Violet," he said, looking back at Milo.

"No, I want to talk about you first. You see, I want you to go away. So I'm gonna give you one more chance. Maybe you are here just looking after Violet. Hey, Lonelyheart? Well, here's your chance to forget her. She never wanted you around anyhow."

"Maybe I heard it a little different, Milo. Maybe she told me she wanted to see me."

"Was that before or after you did her?"

"I didn't kill her."

"Not what I hear, Gander. People talk. You know what they say?"

"What people?"

"They say she was gonna meet you just about that time."

"I never touched her."

"And they saw her hanging around outside your place just before it happened, and maybe she even sent you a letter."

"Who said? The guy you planted in the newsstand?"

"And the letter said to meet her." Milo smiled. "Guess where?"

Gander waited.

"At the carousel. This don't look so good, Harvey." Milo spread his hands to illustrate the dilemma, the gun pointing like a short black finger. "But you see, I'm giving you a chance here. You can go away. You can forget you ever heard about her."

"Where's the Sultan? I want to talk to him."

"Fat chance."

"You listen to me, Milo."

"No!" snapped Milo, angry now. "*You* listen. You keep comin' around and you are gonna get hurt. You hear me?"

"Did you kill her, Milo?"

"Fuck you, Gander. She was crap. She was nothin'."

"I'm gonna find out. I'm gonna paste it all over page one. I'm gonna paste your picture all over there with it."

"Oh a story, is that it? Like your buddy? What's his name? Martin? You'll get the same sweet shit he did, Gander."

Gander stood in place, the words meaningless, then registering seconds later, like a gunshot.

"You didn't," Gander said.

"What'd you think? It was some *heart* attack? Loved the obituary, pal."

And then Milo was speaking, his mouth open, but Gander couldn't make out the words. Something inside him was pulling away, as though it were not his own life but some other man's and he was watching. He floated far above the room, staring down at two small men, him and Milo, with Natasha alone, tied up and sitting on the bed.

He could feel it all shifting back downward when something exploded.

Gander knocked Milo up and backward off his feet, sent him sprawling to the floor. He stalked after him, stood straddled over him, reached down and wrenched the pistol away, aiming it at Milo's face, Milo screaming silently, *No! No!* mouth open, arms recoiling snakelike to cover his face. Gander threw the pistol across the floor, knelt down and clutched Milo's hair, pounded Milo's head against the tiles, over and over, stamping spongy red blotches onto the black and white squares.

Gander stumbled backward, his chest heaving. "Damn you!" he whispered at the still body, blood trickling down its neck. He placed his hands over his face, twisting his palms into his sockets, his blurred eyes focusing on the mirror, his reflection, and, beyond it, like a ghost, Natasha Nyle floating toward him.

"Harvey."

He swung around. She was there, facing him, her eyes black and wide.

"You *untied* yourself!" he exclaimed.

"I can't believe you did that."

"You *untied* yourself!"

"Yeah," she answered vaguely. "Fake knots." Then, remembering, she slipped off a white cord still braceleting her left wrist. "All they wanted was to scare you a little."

Gander barking like a dog: *"What's going on here?"*

"I told you. They wanted to scare you a little. Poor Milo."

Gander opened his mouth to speak but closed it. He could find nothing to say. He walked to the mirror, leaned into it, and slid down against the glass, crouching on his heels, the reflection of Natasha Nyle's long white legs rising beside him. She bent slightly at the waist, hands on hips, looking down at Milo, but at that moment Milo's chest heaved, his eyelids fluttered, and he began to snore violently. Natasha drew back. She turned to Gander, a hand on a hip. "He's breathing."

"So I hear."

"Well, what are you going to do when he wakes up? He'll be *furious.*"

Gander slid up against the mirror to face her. "I'm getting out of here."

Natasha approached. "Harvey, what about *me?*" she said. A finger pointing at her chest.

"But first I'm gonna tie up your friend," Gander said and walked past her across the room to the bed. He gathered the short lengths of rope she'd left scattered on the spread.

Gander rolled Milo over onto his stomach, muffling the snores, and spread the hair at the back of his head to look at the wound, a pair of short gashes, the blood already clotting. He bound Milo's wrists together behind his back, coiled a stretch of white rope around his ankles, and used Natasha Nyle's white blindfold as a gag. He stood up and studied his work, Milo's face flat and lifeless against the tiles. He looked over at Natasha. "Maybe I should put him on the bed," he considered. She stood before the mirror in her bra and slip, studying herself.

"What for?" she said to her reflection.

Gander shrugged and walked over to stand beside her.

She posed, slightly sideways, looking across her shoulder at her body in profile, Gander at her side.

"They sure wanted you down here," she said to her reflection.

"Pardon me?" he answered hers.

"Down here," she repeated. "They wanted you down here."

Gander leaned toward the mirror, peering in, his face going close to the glass. "The mirror," he said.

"What about it?"

"There's someone *in* there," he said, his face pressed against his reflection, his voice dropping. He stepped heavily back. "Someone is *in* there."

"*So?*"

"They watched me attack him." He grabbed her by the shoulders. "They saw me *attack* him."

"Hey, watch it!"

Gander shoved her aside and knelt beside Milo's body, rooting through his trouser pockets. He found the keys and turned to confront her, whispering, "You're coming with me."

"Oh, I don't know, Harvey. They won't be real happy about that."

"Natasha," he reasoned, sliding out of his jacket, "look what they did to Violet. Here. Put this on."

"Why?" A half smile. "Embarrassed?"

"Just put it on. Unless you want to wear his suit." Gesturing at Milo.

"No, thanks," she answered, slipping into the jacket.

Gander said, "Quick. Turn around." She spun in place. "Okay. We go."

He took her hand and led her from the room, back down the hallway to the janitor's closet, steered her inside and closed the door behind them. He stared at the open fuse box. "How do you make it go up?"

She shook her head. "I don't know what you're talking about. What are we doing in this *closet*?"

"How did *you* get down here?"

"To the basement? We used the stairs behind the mirror."

He pressed the buttons he had pushed to make it go down. Underneath the elevator something clicked, but they waited, not moving, in silence. He smacked his palm against the fuses. The machinery clicked. The elevator hummed and started to rise.

"It's an elevator!" said Natasha.

"You tried to call me this morning," Gander said, the door dropping away.

"I know. I felt bad about Violet."

"What do you know about her?"

"Nothing."

"Who was back there behind the mirror?"

"Nobody."

"Natasha, this is not helpful."

"I'm not sure this is such a good idea," she answered.

The door that led back into High Water dropped from above. Voices on the other side spoke in the distance, maybe as far away as the bar itself. But the door kept dropping and the little room continued to rise.

"What's upstairs?" Gander asked.

"The theater," she said.

He looked at his watch. "Nine-thirty. It can't be nine-thirty. I forgot to call Patty."

"Patty who?"

A second door descended from the ceiling and came to a stop before them.

"Where are we? Is this the theater?"

She shrugged and watched him turn the doorknob to peer out. Another empty hallway.

"Wait here, okay?"

She nodded and he walked quickly away down the hall, pausing at the far end to look around the corner, then slip from sight. Natasha stepped out and let the door close behind her. She leaned back against it as it locked with a click. A minute passed. Gears turned behind the door. She placed her ear flat against it, listening as the elevator descended. Down the shaft another door opened and two talking men stepped on, their voices muffled. Then one voice said, "Gander," clearly. The elevator was moving again. She waited without breathing until one of them spoke, far down the shaft.

Gander reappeared at the far end of the hall, beckoning. When she was close enough for whispering, he said, "Wear this," and unwrapped a man's beige raincoat from his arm. He shook it and held it open. She slipped out of his jacket, turned her back to him, and slid her arms down the sleeves of the raincoat.

"Nice! Where'd you get it?"

"The coat room. My wife took sick and I can't find my ticket."

"Harvey, the elevator went back down. Some men got on and they're going down to the basement."

They turned together, looking down the hallway at the closed door. Arm in arm they walked away toward the lobby, but as they passed a telephone Gander held back. "This'll just take a second," he said.

He lifted the loose batch of messages from his jacket pocket, but they slipped from his hand and floated to the floor like leaves. Gander and Natasha sank to their heels to gather them, Gander's hands rummaging haphazardly through the lot. "Here it is," he said and looked up. Natasha sat on her heels, the raincoat wide, her knees wide. He glanced back over his shoulder. A man standing in a doorway stared bug-eyed at her crotch. Gander stared back and the man disappeared.

"You're a full-time job, you know that?" Gander said as they stood.

"What's the matter?"

"Nothing. Button your coat."

"Sure, but I don't think you should be calling anybody right now, Harvey."

"I have to."

"Then maybe I should go back and watch the elevator?"

"Yes, yes."

He was out of nickels. He dropped in a quarter and dialed Patty's number.

"Hello?" she answered.

"Patty. It's Harvey."

"Is something wrong, or have I been stood up?"

"Patty, I'm sorry. I didn't know what time it was. Honest. But I need to know. Did you find out who bought High Water?"

"Ooh, Mr. Romance. Yes, I found out, but I don't know whether it's . . ."

Natasha flew around the corner. "Harvey! They're coming!"

He waited a fraction of a second, then: "Patty. Don't ask. Go to my place. *Now.*"

He grabbed Natasha's hand, the receiver bouncing against the wall behind them, and they ran through the open front doors of the theater, the beige raincoat spreading like wings behind Natasha's long white legs. A young couple on the sidewalk jumped back, the man shouting angrily after them as they poured into the street. A cab skidded to a stop and they piled in.

"*Go!*"

The taxicab lurched away, throwing them back against the seat. "Turn! *Anywhere.* HERE!"

The car squealed around the corner, Gander hanging on to a hand strap. He looked back through the rear window to the empty theater entrance. No one was behind them. They hadn't been seen.

The Harem

They leaned against one another in the dark, headed north on Fullsome.

"Can I ask you something, Harvey?"

"Why not."

"Why are we going to your place?"

"Because I have to feed my kitten. Because I told a girl to meet me there."

"They'll come after us, is all."

"I don't think so. There was someone behind the mirror. I saw him. I don't know what to think."

"No, they'll come. They're just going to want me, maybe."

"I'll take you to the train station. You can be out of town in an hour."

"No. An hour I don't mind. It's all the time after that."

They rode, and she lay her head on his shoulder, her white leg splitting the skirt of the raincoat and rising up to rest on his knee.

"Who's the girl?" she asked.

"Just a girl I know."

"Why's she coming over?"

Gander looked into her face. "Because I asked her to." Natasha looked out the window.

"Well, what's all the fuss about anyway?" she said, watching the passing buildings.

"That's what you're going to tell me."

"Tell you what?"

"What all the fuss is about. Do you know who Paul York is?"

"No, who's he?"

"He gave me an assignment to write about the Superlative Man, and everything came unglued."

"Maybe it was a coincidence," she said.

Her leg slid away from Gander's knee and she leaned back, her eyes wide and staring at oncoming lights.

Patty was already waiting in the vestibule when they climbed the steps from the curb. Across the street, the newsstand was dark.

She said, "Harvey," looking at Natasha, "you scared me half to death with that business on the phone. What's going on?"

"I shouldn't have told you to come, Patty. I wasn't thinking."

Patty looking at Natasha in the beige raincoat and bare feet.

"Well, I suppose if I've interrupted . . ." she started.

"It isn't that. Natasha, tell her it isn't that."

Natasha looked sideways at Patty.

"Thank you, Natasha," said Harvey. "All right. Who knows. Maybe I'm right. Maybe they won't come after us. Anyway, the newsstand over there is closed up for the night."

"Well, that makes all the sense in the world," Patty observed as Gander unlocked the inside door.

"Which ain't much," he answered, holding it open.

Gander never turned on the kitchen light. Patty and Natasha sat in the dark, the kitten crouched between them on the table, lapping milk. Gander stood at the window, a long shadow looking down at the street.

"So who bought High Water?" he asked.

"A little company nobody ever heard of," Patty answered. "It was about a year ago."

"Called?"

"High Water Properties."

The kitten walked to the edge of the table and lay on its belly, its paws curling over the rim.

"Who owns it?"

"There's no name listed. The woman I talked to couldn't explain. She said there was something wrong."

Gander walked back to the table. "Natasha. Did the Sultan buy it?"

She nodded. "He knows who you are."

"That's nice. Who *is* he?"

"It's his place. He owns it. But there are all these other men around these days, like Karl and Milo. They don't like you, Harvey. It's why they're trying to scare you away. And now you've gone and practically beaten Milo to death."

"Harvey!" Patty exclaimed.

"Patty, forget it. Natasha. Listen to me. This matters. I'm not asking you. I need to know why Violet was killed."

Natasha picked up the kitten and held it against her chest. "Karl didn't like her. He thinks she talked too much about the accidents."

"The rescues?"

Natasha nodded. "We sort of staged them," she said. "But you knew that already. After you left my apartment yesterday, I telephoned them and told them you knew. Were they ever *furious!*"

"Harvey," Patty interrupted again. She was staring at Gander. "You *beat* a man?"

"You shouldn't be here," he said to her.

"Tonight?"

Down on the street a car door slammed.

"All right," he said, shaking his head, walking back to the window. "Here we go."

A second door slammed.

He turned to face them, his figure a silhouette against the glass. "We shouldn't be here. I made a mistake."

"I told you, Harvey," said Natasha. "They're looking for me. It was the same with Violet. They don't like it when you leave."

Three flights below, the door to the vestibule burst open, the noise ripping up the stairwell.

"Shut up, shut up," Gander said, his voice tight. "Don't panic. Just don't *panic*. Patty. Patty, look at me. Take off your clothes."

"*What!*"

"Shut up! There isn't time. Natasha, into the bedroom. Now!"

He pulled Patty out of the chair by her shoulders. "*Strip!*" he hissed in her face.

Voices whispered in the hallway beyond the living room. Metal rasped at the front door, then a long, empty silence filled the dark. The bedroom door opened and a flashlight beam swung across the room, freezing two figures on the bed. Gander sat up in the light, blocking the woman behind him.

"Who's there?" he shouted angrily in the glare.

"We're takin' the girl." Karl's voice. "You we talk to later."

The beam of light bobbed toward the bed.

"Stay right there," a second voice instructed.

Dime.

Karl said, "Don't move. Just sit there, real quiet." The shadow of his arm reached down to the sheet, yanking it away. Patty sat bolt upright in the light. "Hey!" her arm across her breasts, the other planted in her lap.

"Who's *this*?" Karl demanded, his voice floating away to find Dime. "It's not her," he declared and turned back to Gander. "All right, so where is she?"

"Who, Natasha?"

"Yeah, Natasha."

"I left her at the train station."

A moment of silence. Patty reached down and slowly drew the sheet back up her body.

Something rustled under the bed. The flashlight traced along the carpet and stopped, spotlighting the face peering out.

M'ow.

Dime snorted. "It's a cat."

"Look, Gander," said Karl, "you and me, we got unfinished business. But not now. Later."

"Got a train to catch, so to speak," Dime explained.

Karl snapped, "Shut up, you."

Just before the bedroom door closed, Dime said, "Nice girl."

Gander slipped from the bed and out of the room. At the kitchen window he watched the two men crawl back into their car and drive away. He reappeared at the bedroom door, naked, and walked across the room through the shadows to the fire escape. Opening the window, he reached out and offered Natasha his hand.

"I'm sorry, Patty," he said, looking back. She sat in the silver light, the sheet drawn up over her breasts. "Look at it this way," he suggested. He sat beside her on the edge of the bed. "They didn't find Natasha."

"Some first date," she answered.

Natasha started toward the kitchen, but stopped and blurted from the doorway, "Put your *pants* on, Harvey," and as she left the room broke into giddy laughter.

Patty watched him in the low light as he went to the closet, took a bathrobe from a hanger, and carried it in front of him back to the bed. He held it out. She slipped to the edge of the bed and stood, turning quickly, the sheet tight in front of her, sliding her arms one at a time into the sleeves of the robe, the sheet falling away to the floor.

. . .

They sat at the kitchen table, Patty in his bathrobe, Gander in his trousers, Natasha in the beige raincoat at the window, watching the street. "Doesn't anybody want a drink?" she said.

"I'd like a drink," Patty said.

"There's beer in the fridge," Gander offered.

Natasha asked, "No liquor?"

"Scotch. In the cupboard over the sink."

Patty pulled an ice tray from the fridge. She opened cupboards until she found one with three glasses. Then she started opening more cupboards as though she just wanted to see what was inside.

"The cupboard over the sink," said Gander.

She reached up, her body arching against the bathrobe. "Whiskey," she said.

"Whiskey," Natasha repeated. "What's your secret, Harvey? Now she's pouring drinks for you."

"I don't know. Patty, what's my secret?"

Patty turned, a hand on her hip, but with a glance at Natasha she turned back to the three drinks without a word.

Natasha joined them at the table and they clinked glasses. Then her face went flat. "Where did you get that?"

She was talking to Gander. He held the little stone man, turning it over in his hand. "What? This?"

"Yes, *this*. Where did you get it?"

"Violet left it in my apartment yesterday."

"When?"

"Natasha, easy. I don't know. Six? Six-thirty?"

"What's the matter, Natasha?" Patty said. She reached out and laid her hand on Natasha's.

"I gave it to her," Natasha said.

All three looked at the tiny carving.

Gander said, "When?"

"Yesterday, after you left my apartment."

"She left it when she left the kitten," Gander said.

"It's like a mark," Natasha tried to explain. "It means you haven't got a whole lot of time left."

Patty and Harvey looked at each other. They looked at Natasha.

"And you gave it to her?" Gander asked.

"Karl told me to. When I told him you knew about the rescues, he realized Violet told you. I didn't want to give it to her. I liked Violet. But maybe she thought she was supposed to give it to you. Maybe that's what she was thinking because she didn't seem real upset when I gave it to her. Although she was funny that way."

"Yeah, hilarious," Gander said. "Real hilarious when we found her, too."

"I heard you were there," Natasha answered.

Gander stood the little statue on the table. "Natasha, what's going on at High Water?"

She picked up the carving and held it beside her face. She smiled broadly. "See? Made for each other," she said.

Harvey and Patty watched her.

She set it on the table facing her. "I told you. Karl made me give it to her. Ever since he came around, everything's changed. It's all money now, nothing but money. It's so odious."

Gander said, "I thought High Water belonged to the Sultan."

"It does. But he let Karl into the business and the others started showing up. All they wanted was the business. Before they came around, it was just like Candy Land."

"Candy Land."

"Honest. You could have anything you wanted. I felt like a little girl. It was wonderful."

"No kidding."

"All they wanted in return was for us to help them with the rescues."

"To stage them."

Natasha nodded. "But now Karl wants to stop doing them. He's afraid people will catch on."

"That they're phony?" Gander finished for her.

"Karl says they're a threat to the business."

"What *is* the business?" Gander asked. "High Water Properties?"

But she said, "It never was just a business for him. He makes them purely for pleasure."

"The drugs? The Sultan *makes* them?"

She nodded.

"That's the *business*?"

"The Sultan's a genius. He can do anything. Every woman who walks into the place falls in love with him. The boys all stay for the money and then are afraid to leave. Even Karl is afraid of the Sultan."

"He makes the drugs at High Water?"

"No, not High Water. Down at the Harem. He makes them, and then he gives them women's names."

"The Harem," Gander echoed.

Natasha beamed. "It's what the Sultan calls it. It's his Harem."

Patty turned to Gander, her eyes wide.

Out in the living room a door latch closed.

"Shh!"

Gander crept barefoot to the kitchen door and looked back over his shoulder. Natasha was whispering to Patty, her mouth up close against Patty's ear. Gander pushed through.

Patty and Natasha watched the door swing shut. A lamp clicked, and a thin band of light shone at the base.

A man's voice said, "Hello, Gander."

Gander answered, "Hello yourself, Elmo."

. . .

Elmo Jade stood beside the lamp, the light making his black eyes shine. Gander waited, his hands in his trouser pockets.

"I heard some talk, Gander."

"What about?"

"I heard there's been trouble."

"Go on, I'm listening."

"They found a fellow down at High Water. He was all in. They found him tied up in the basement."

"Tough luck."

"I heard you were down there, too."

"I'm starting to think you know these people real well, Jade."

"It was you?"

"Maybe it was just a coincidence," Gander suggested.

"I don't think they're coming after you for it. I wanted to tell you that. But you shouldn't have walked off with Natasha."

"Somebody beat you to this, Jade. They searched the place. Nothing. I don't know what you're talking about."

"Maybe. I also heard she might have on a man's raincoat." Gander concentrated on keeping his face from changing. "Mind if I stick around?" Jade asked.

"Yeah, I mind."

"Okay. Then you're going to have to turn around and put your hands in your back pockets. This'll only take a minute."

Gander had waited for it. He had not wanted to see it. Not from Jade. But he'd waited. And for the third time that day he stared at the black hollow point of a gun.

"You got to trust me on this one, Gander. You don't know half of what's going on. And you don't need to. Except that you should stay away from Natasha. Go on back into the kitchen."

Jade was flat up behind him when Gander pushed through the kitchen door. A single light shone over the stove. Patty stood in front of it, facing them in the beige raincoat, her eyes locked on Jade's. He opened his mouth to speak and the point of a knife pierced the back of his jacket, touching his skin.

"Give the gun to Harvey," Natasha said.

Gander spun around and took the gun, Jade letting it go without a word. Natasha stood close behind Jade, the bathrobe tied loosely at her waist.

And then Jade was talking over his shoulder, his words fast together. "Natasha. You don't know me. I'm Elmo Jade. I can help you. I know people who can get you away."

"I think it's none of your business, Elmo Jade," she answered. "Harvey, keep him here until you see me get in a cab?" She smiled a thin smile, backed through the door, and was gone.

"Gander," Jade said. "Just listen."

"Why don't you shut up, Jade," Gander answered and walked away to the window.

She appeared on the street, waving up at the window. She turned and waved at a passing cab. A man walking his dog on the opposite sidewalk stopped to watch her in her bathrobe and bare feet. She waved at him, too. When she was gone, Gander walked over to the table and lay the pistol next to the kitchen knife.

"Okay," he said.

"You know where she's going?" Jade said.

"I don't care where she's going."

"Maybe you should. She's going back to High Water."

"Let her."

"This was her chance to get away."

"What are you talking about, Jade? I thought you came here to take her back."

"She needs help, Gander. When I heard they came looking and didn't find her, I thought maybe she's hiding, maybe she's ready to leave High Water."

"She's going back?"

"She's cold around the edges. She's hooked. They all are."

"On what?"

"Oh, come on, man, did you even *look* at her? *Drugs*, Gander. They got her all tangled up down there. But they do that to people. Look at you. You didn't want to get mixed up in this. But wait. They'll hook you, too. They're playing with you. Ever since you wrote that obituary for Martin they've had their eye on you."

"Martin's obituary," Gander spoke to the floor. He looked up at Jade. "They killed him."

Jade looked genuinely startled.

"Hey," said Gander, "I finally get a rise out of you."

Jade placed a hand flat on the swinging door. "I'm just surprised you found that out. Gander, listen," he said, "I have to go. I'm sorry about the gun."

Gander stared back at him, then pointed at the pistol lying on the table.

Jade slipped the handgun into his pocket.

"She's going back?" Gander said.

"Yes."

"Maybe you were right. Maybe I shouldn't have let her go."

Jade said, "She's been places you never even thought of," and walked out the door.

Missing Pieces

They stood beside the kitchen table, Patty leaning against him. "Those people," she said. "I could barely talk as long as those people were here. And that *woman*. I don't even *want* to know."

"I found her at High Water."

"What's going on, Harvey? You shouldn't be mixed up with these people."

He moved down onto a kitchen chair, taking her hand, pulling her to the chair beside him.

"Did you really beat up a man?" she asked.

"Martin didn't die of a heart attack, Patty. They killed him. When I found out, I just lost it."

"So many people getting killed. I'm scared."

"I'm scared, too," he said. "Patty, stay here with me."

"Oh, Harvey. No."

"I don't want to be alone."

She looked down at her raincoat, at her hands in her lap, at the table, at the window.

"Patty?"

She looked up at him.

"Stay here with me," he said.

And she leaned into him.

. . .

When they walked into the bedroom, he never turned on the lights. They never pulled down the sheets. And Patty never got out of the beige raincoat, standing by the bed, Gander's trousers at his right ankle, his lips pressed against hers, gently and then harder. He pulled her to him, his hands skating across the cotton surface of her coat, his hand slipping flat under the fold onto her bare stomach, her lips moving in a sharp intake across his cheek and past his ear. Her knee rose against him, splitting the skirt, her tongue at a point and touching his ear, and a hard arc against her. She lay her palm against him and he made a soft sound, looking down her body, naked under the coat, his hand tracing across her breasts and dropping to her sex, his fingers curling through her hair, touching her, and she pushed hard against him, their mouths together, Gander falling backward toward the bed, Patty falling after. He held her hips, touching her wet core, and they drifted into each other, deliberate, slow, a circular wave that crested, broke, and spread like silence through the room.

"Oh no." Words like two smoke rings.
  "What," Gander said. "What."
  "The curtains. We never closed the curtains."
Through the open window across the street, a woman stood framed in her apartment window. He crawled along the floor on his hands and knees, drew the curtains gently to a close.

Pillows piled behind them, they lay together in the darkened room, Patty curved naked against him, her cheek on his breast, his arm curled around her shoulders. She breathed quietly, asleep, her breast rising and falling into his cupped hand.
  He couldn't sleep. He couldn't even close his eyes, his thoughts racing places he did not want to go. He slid silently away in the

silver light, and she didn't wake. Until his knee tapped against the bedside table, rattled a drawer handle, and she murmured.

He whispered, "It's all right. Go back to sleep."

"I want . . ."

"What? Want what?"

She rose on one elbow, looking for him in the shadow, her voice small, like a child's. "I want my fairy queendom."

"You *what*?"

"I want my fairy king—my fairy . . . I want . . ."

"Shh. You're dreaming. Shh." He held her in his arms and she fell back to sleep.

The slow rise and fall of her breathing, the only sound when he walked into the bathroom and closed the door, turned on the light, and winced in the ugly glare. Behind the shower curtain lay the soap dish, a washcloth. A final glimpse of his head and arm leaning awkwardly in front of the mirror as he reached for the light.

He never did get to the soap, standing in the hot rush of water, his ears all noise, something emptying out of him, the hard spray streaming against his face, sweating into the steaming rinse, a thousand corruptions pouring down the drain.

Maybe it was the dark, or the heat of the water, or maybe it was because the day would not end but kept pouring on into the night, but the image of her body recurred and recurred—her breasts lifting, her back arching, her hair down—and he wanted her again, and again, on the bed, in the shower, in his arms. He wanted her naked and sleepy on the edge of dreamland; he wanted to lather her awake in the steaming rinse; he wanted his naked fairy queen awake with longing and he did not want to let go.

He stood naked at the window, the curtain wide, the window wide, his mind crowded with voices. So much had happened. So fast. It had all come unloosed with the ride to the pier. Or maybe it was at Philippa Fife's. But something had happened. Before that, it was as though he weren't really a part of the story. It wouldn't have mattered if he had just stopped and walked away. But he was caught now in this swirling tide, and all that mattered was to touch down somewhere, anywhere, to take Patty and just go. All he wanted was some quiet place, insulated from the spiraling chaos.

In the apartment across the street the woman walked past a window. She passed a second window and the rooms went black behind her. An airplane droned high overhead, then faded beyond an intervening range of buildings. In the kitchen the telephone rang. Then a passing silence. Only the sound of water dripping in the bathroom. The woman stood in her dark window, staring back across the street at Gander's empty building.

In the bedroom he dressed in the dark, leaned over Patty's sleeping figure lying curled beneath the sheet. He tucked the sheet around her and drew the bedroom door to a close, silently turning the knob. At the kitchen phone, he dialed Jade's home number.

"What."

"It's Gander."

"Where are you?"

"I need to talk."

"Okay. Where?"

"There's an all-night diner on Carridge."

"I'll be there."

"You know it?"

"Yeah, it's around the corner from me."

"Give me fifteen minutes," Gander said.

"Don't walk. Take a cab."

"I'm walking. I'll be there in fifteen minutes," Gander said and hung up.

. . .

The streets were quiet. A cab stalked a tired window shopper under scattered lights. Gander walked two blocks west, turned south another three, and slowed as he approached the next corner, listening to footsteps behind him. He quickened his pace, burst into a sprint, but just around the corner, stopped short, leaning up close against the side of the building, his reflection pale beside him in dark plate glass. Rapid footsteps rose behind him, careening around the corner and stopping dead in two brown shoes, a loose brown suit, and a thin tired face under a low hat.

"Hiya, Dime," Gander said.

"Gander. A true surprise. You'll excuse me if I have a train to catch."

"Station's the other way."

"So it is. So it is. Seems like just this morning you and I had a nice chat. But what are you doin' out so late? Lookin' for somebody?"

"Should I be?"

"I don't know. Thought maybe you were lookin' for somebody."

"What is it with you guys? What do you want with me?"

"Don't kid yourself. Couldn't care if you live or die."

"Then why are you tailing me?"

"That's funny," Dime said, his face nodding. "I'm catching a train."

"Out doing the little jobs nobody else wants to?"

"Back off, Jack."

"Maybe it was you they told to do Violet."

"You talk too much, Gander."

"And Martin, too. It was you, wasn't it?"

"I mean it, pal. I don't care what they say, you keep up this funny stuff and you are dead."

"What *do* they say?"

"I'm telling you what *I* say."

"What are you in it for? Is it the drugs? Or just the money?"

"You wait, Gander. One day they'll have you good."

"I just wondered what your soft spot was."

"They'll do you. You'll scare. And I'll be there to see it."

"So scare me."

"Sorry," Dime smiled. "You ain't my type."

"What's the matter? Too old?"

Dime's hands never moved. He leaped at Gander head first. Gander's arms flew up to meet him, but he had no chance to brace himself and toppled backward, his head landing against the pavement. A muffled thud. Dime clutched Gander's hair with tight fists, hammering his head against the pavement. Thud. Thud. Sounds fell out of sequence. Thud. Tires screeched. Coarse shouting and rattling fire. Dime flying backward through space, through the dark plate glass and the shattering reflection of Gander's pale face.

On hands and knees, hovering above the sidewalk. Something tickles his cheek, runs down his chin, dripping there. The kitten padding into view, lapping at the spreading dark pool. Two black shoes patter by and frighten it away. Overhead somebody cracks a home run.

A hand brushes his forehead. He no longer hovers on his hands and knees. He is on his back, staring at the stars, a pale hand moving through them, shuffling them there. A white planet rolls toward a corner pocket, slows, hesitates, then slips over the edge into a black hole. The kitten's face peers out, the white planet balanced on its head. Gander sits up reaching for it and tumbles headlong into space.

A voice, low and murmuring. A drifting bed, like a leaf on water. But it tilts, as though at any moment he might slide off feet first.

The voice low, murmuring. One voice. Talking. Then silent. Gander opens his mouth to speak: "Whuh." But the effort upsets a delicate balance. He can feel himself sliding away.

On a bed. On a bed leaning back. Leaning back against a brace of pillows. I am sitting on a bed.

He swallows. Rolling rocks.

Light in a room. Low golden light. And a shadow: a single voice, soft and distinct.

"He's coming 'round."

Gander peered out through his lashes at the shadow in the corner, his lids weighted, the soft light blurring.

"Easy, Gander. Easy does it."

Please don't make me move. Please. Don't make me move.

Something cold, wet, and dark washed over his face, dripped down his cheeks and neck into the pillows. Gander touched a finger to his left ear, and his entire body shuddered. His eyes opened slow and cold.

"Hey now. No touching, all right?"

"Jade."

"Yeah. How are you?"

His hat back, his tie loose, white sleeves rolled up to the elbows, Elmo Jade leaned over the bed looking down at Gander.

"Where are we?"

"My place."

"What time is it?"

"Almost two. How's your head? You lost a little blood."

"I can't tell. You brought me here?"

Jade nodded.

"I don't get it."

"I went out looking for you. I told you, you shouldn't be out tonight."

"Dime," Gander said.

"What about him?"

"Last thing I remember, he was pounding my head against a sidewalk."

"You never saw him."

"Say it again."

"You dreamed it."

"I don't get you, Jade. I don't get you at all."

"You don't need to. I'm just a reporter who keeps tabs on undertown."

Gander's hand rose toward his ear but Jade intercepted it. "Don't touch. I mean it."

"I want a mirror."

"It's wrapped."

"I want a mirror."

"Why don't you have a drink first."

"What's wrong with my *ear*?"

"A piece of it's missing."

Jade left the room. When he returned, he carried half a bottle of whiskey and a glass. Gander put the mouth of the bottle to his lips and sipped. The liquor scorched his throat.

"Water," he rasped.

Jade left. In another room a tap ran. Ice cubes clinked against glass. He reappeared holding out a dripping highball. Gander drank the water in long swallows, then upended the bottle of whiskey. His eyes watered and he breathed noisily.

The phone was ringing, Jade answering it: "Wait a minute."

Gander sat on the edge of the bed.

Jade said, "Where are you going?"

"Bathroom."

"Yeah? Why you taking the bottle?"

"For balance," Gander answered, and then in a singsong: "Everything but everything is in balance."

Jade spoke into the telephone. "Wait a minute."

Gander tied his shoes, looking up. "Kind of slippery, this floor. You need carpet." Tying his shoes, his fingers wads of clay.

"Just give me a couple minutes in here," Jade said. "I'll be right out."

Gander shuffled into the living room and Jade closed the bedroom door behind him. His bloodstained jacket lay draped over the back of a chair. His misshapen hat sat next to it on the seat. He folded the jacket over one arm, picked up his hat, and walked away across the living-room floor, out the front door, and into the building's lobby. Sliding on his jacket and setting his hat at an angle away from his left ear, he ventured out into the empty street.

The air was light and cool. He waited in the middle of the street, sipping at the whiskey. At the next corner a cab rolled across the intersection. Gander beckoned as it disappeared from view. A moment passed and it reappeared, backing into the intersection, turning toward him. It approached up the pavement and Gander stumbled across the busy surface of a manhole cover, opened the door, and fell in.

The cabbie turned, looking back over the seat. "Just drive," Gander said, his face against the cushion.

Jade, he thought. Elmo Jade.

"Where to?" the cabbie said, his lips wet, protruding, his eyes withdrawn.

"Go north, go south, go in circles, I don't care."

"Sure, sure." His head not moving. "You okay?"

"I feel fine." Gander looked at the bottle in his hand.

Twenty minutes later it was empty and he felt less. The night was clear, surfaces hard. The cabbie turned onto Third Avenue, paced the lights, and rolled through one green intersection after another, green, red, and yellow lights blinking on up the avenue. Gander stared out the window at passing windows.

Elmo Jade. Mr. Everywhere. Who is he? My guardian angel? The fifth name on my list?

A crack reporter who doesn't believe in coincidence.

But I called him. I *called* him.

He believes in evil. He said that. Then he covers for Dime. "You never saw him, Gander." Maybe he's covering for the whole damn lot of them. He talks like he knows every last one.

It's all too snug.

He was there at the carousel. Then with Natasha at my apartment, he knew all about it. He knows what's happening as soon as it happens, but tells me some things and doesn't tell me others. He goes and covers for Dime, then hands me drinks to bring me around.

You can't play both sides of the fence.

Or maybe he's just sitting on the fence.

Everything is doubling.

Like the Superlative Man, saving some people and not others.

Or like me.

Gander reached up under his hat, touching his fingers to the soft wound at the back of his head. When he saw him.

The Superlative Man
    Glimpsed down a side street
    In the middle of the street

His cape hanging down behind, curling at his calf, like a quote. His legs a tall triangle. His thick arms akimbo, fists planted on hips. The ivory-colored *S* and *M* bold, curving, spreading across his scarlet chest. His face jutting, solid and carved. His eyes flashing. A dark curl of hair at his forehead, like a quote.

"Stop the car!"

The cabbie slammed on the brakes and Gander sailed face first into the back of the front seat.

His hand rose to cover his face. "My nose," he said. "It's bleeding."

"Hey, you say stop, I stop."

"*Back up!* To the intersection." Gander turned and stared out the rear window as the corner of a building slid away and the side street opened again before them. The empty side street.

"Where to, Mac?"

Gander leaned his head back against the seat, looking up through the rear window to the dark sky, its few stars.

"Where to, buddy?"

Where to.

"Remember where you picked me up?"

"Yeah, I remember."

"Let's go."

"Somehow I figured," the cabbie muttered.

But the lights were out at Jade's, empty dark windows over the street. The lone yellow cab crouched at a pool of lamp light, purring.

"Twelve-fifteen." The cabbie mouthing words at his windshield.

"What?"

"You owe me twelve-fifteen."

"How long have we been driving?"

"Long enough to run up twelve dollars fifteen cents of my time."

Gander dropped a ten and a five over the seat. "Keep it."

"With pleasure."

He tripped on the curb, caught himself, and glanced back into the cab. The driver swung his eyes and the car crept away, burning bright under the streetlamp, accelerating into darkness, collapsing into speed.

Patty's Dead

Gander started down the sidewalk, balancing his head above his body, careful not to let it drift too far in any one direction. A cab meandered by, slowed to eye him, then wandered away. The blocks stretched hollow and vast at each new corner he turned.

He drifted homeward, oblivious of any intent greater than to reach his bed, crawl in beside Patty, and sleep. But when at last he turned down his own street, a sudden and deep reluctance to go any farther overcame him. It was as spontaneous as instinct. He simply could not face climbing all those stairs to sit alone in his living room and stare sleepless at the dark.

Down the sidewalk, in the fringe of a streetlamp, a soft shadow on his building's stoop resolved into the crisp outline of a dark hat, a face in profile, elbows on knees. Gander lowered himself gingerly onto the step beside Elmo Jade.

"I walked over here from your place," he said.

"I left there to find you," Jade answered.

The street was silent. They spoke in whispers.

"Sorry," Gander said. "I guess I thought I had some place to go."

"Where did you go?"

"I'm not sure exactly. I was trying to get lost, but I ended up back where I started."

"Saw the light, did you?"

Gander looked over at him, but Jade was staring across the street at the shuttered newsstand.

"Maybe," Gander said.

Jade met his eyes. "Glad to hear it," he said and rose to his feet. "C'mon." He looked down at the top of Gander's bandaged head. "Let's get you to bed. You should sleep."

"I've been thinking about you, Jade."

"C'mon. We'll talk as we walk."

They climbed the stairs to the second floor, Gander's right palm curling like a paw on Jade's left shoulder, Jade pacing himself, letting Gander follow.

"How's your head?" Jade asked.

"It's starting to hurt."

"Finish the whiskey?"

Gander looked down at his empty left hand. "I suppose so," he answered.

"Any more upstairs?"

Gander thought and then nodded. "On the kitchen table."

They rounded the banister on the second-floor landing.

"You got a nasty little wound on the back of your head," Jade noted quietly. "I wrapped the bandage."

"What about my ear?" Gander answered. "You said something about my ear."

"I know. A piece of it's missing."

"That's what I thought you said." Gander paused, waiting on the half-landing before climbing the last steps to the third floor. "Is it big?" he asked.

"Is what big?"

"The piece of my ear."

Jade looked at him. "Not very. Just the earlobe."

"What was it? A knife?"

"No, it wasn't a knife."

Gander waited.

"He bit it off, Gander."

Gander opened his mouth to speak. He closed his mouth. He climbed the stairs and Jade closed the gap between them, his hand gripping Gander's upper right arm.

Gander stopped with three steps to go. "I don't like you, Jade," he said.

"You don't have to," Jade answered. "Let's go inside."

Gander turned the key in the lock and felt his way through the dark living room to the standing lamp, the sudden lamplight capturing Jade at the kitchen door as he disappeared through. Curled in a corner of the sofa, the kitten lifted its head, stretched, and stood yawning. Gander scooped it in one hand and held it to his chest, its tiny mouth opening to cry. A sudden rush of love for the little creature seared his heart. He spoke softly, pattering like a mother to a small child. Are you hungry? Was it scary in the dark? Forgetting his wounds, his exhaustion, the gritty resin of alcohol clotting his brain, he talked away to the uncomprehending animal like an idiot boy concentrated on a small and perplexing world.

And he was still talking when he walked through the doorway into his bedroom.

And saw Patty in the moonlight. Stretched out on his bed, naked in the beige raincoat, the coat spread away beneath her like a cape.

He turned on the light.

Blood moved behind his face. He didn't need to go closer, didn't need to touch her.

Her eyes were closed, her mouth covered in blood like badly smeared lipstick, her bared teeth clenched.

He lifted her hand. It dropped back lifeless to the mattress as though weighted. He closed the coat over her and stepped back, pressing the kitten against him, its claws sprouting into his chest, and he just kept walking, backward, leaving the room and turning into the kitchen. On the kitchen table sat the bottle of whiskey. Jade stood at the sink, his back to the door, the water running. Gander lifted the bottle and drank, and he kept drinking, and it could have been warm water for all it burned. Until a high wind struck and his eyes streamed, his head on fire. Somewhere far away he could hear his name: "Gander, Gander," and at first he could not connect the sound to Jade, in front of him, holding him by his shoulders.

But he could hear his own voice: "It's Patty," he said. "They killed her," the words foreign and repulsive. Jade bolted from the kitchen, Gander following slowly. In the bedroom Jade hovered over the bed. Gander knelt beside him.

And saw it.

A soft pulp between stained teeth. A tiny bulb.

Clenched.

And he knew.

His throat opened and the noise poured out at her. Hot streaming tears burned his face. And the kitten's claws sank deeper and he pressed the animal tighter.

As tight as the lobe of ear in the teeth of his deposed queen.

He careened off the door frame into the living room, stopping in place, mindlessly tossing the kitten onto the sofa and heading to the kitchen. Jade intercepted him at the swinging door. "No you don't. You can't drink now. I'm calling the police."

"I'm not drunk."

"Keep it that way."

Jade banged through the kitchen door and Gander walked away to the living-room window to stare at the street. He could hear Jade talking into the receiver. "Yeah. Officer Carter. Can I leave a message and he'll get it? Okay. Elmo Jade. Tell Carter I need him. There's a girl dead. I'm at 2007 Seventh Avenue. Yeah, I'll wait."

Jade pushed through. "Gander, you and I need to talk."

"I did this," Gander said.

"Careful now."

"I did this to her."

"Cut the crap. You've been set up. She was here with you. Now she's dead and she's got a piece of ear in her teeth. You, my friend, are missing a piece of your ear."

"Dime did this."

"And you gotta forget Dime, too. Trust me on this one."

"He killed her. He tried to kill me."

"Maybe so." And incongruously, spastically, Jade's face spread into a wicked grin. "Maybe he was just trying to eat you."

Gander sat on the sofa, the kitten beside him standing motionless on the cushion where he had tossed it, as though planted there. He scratched its forehead and its eyes widened.

When he spoke, it was low and to the kitten. "I made love to her and now they'll think I killed her."

"Cops like easy answers," Jade interrupted. He stood by the swinging door, his hands shoved in his jacket, stretching the pockets, his hat back on his head, his forehead glistening. "That's why I called them. They need to hear from us before we hear from them. If they haven't been tipped already."

"You're sweating," Gander answered accusingly.

"Damn right I am."

"You were waiting here for me."

"So *I* killed her?" Jade shot back. "While you were out getting lost I came over here and did her? Oh, and yeah. First I went and found your ear and stuffed it in her mouth."

"I hate you. Oh, man, I hate you."

"This has Karl all over it. It's just like Violet. They set you up, Gander."

Jade disappeared into the kitchen. When he walked back into the room he was carrying the bottle of scotch. He sat down in the chair facing Gander and sipped the liquor.

"Who was that you asked for on the phone?" Gander said.

"One of the cops who came along in Carnival Park, the night we found Violet."

"Last night, damn it. It was last night."

"I called him today to see if they found anything. His name's Carter and we know some of the same people."

"And?"

"Not much. But his partner, a guy named Black, he has it figured as a hit."

"What do you know."

Jade set the bottle on the carpet next to his chair. He stood and walked away toward the bedroom.

"Where do you think you're going?"

"To the girl," Jade said, not looking back. "We need to get rid of that ear."

Gander reached abruptly for the kitten and it shrank back. He scraped it up in his hands and settled it in his lap. He could hear Jade moving about the bedroom. Water ran. Then a long, dead pause.

"Jade?" Gander called.

"Jade?" he said.

Jade appeared in the doorway. "I think you better come in here."

"No way."

"I mean it. Come in here."

"No, I said."

"Gander. She's not dead."

Gander stood in place, his bandaged head canted to one side, the kitten dangling from his left hand.

"She's not," Jade repeated.

The kitten dropped to the floor and scrambled away.

"How do you mean that?" Gander inquired.

"I mean she isn't not breathing."

"But I *saw* her."

"So did I. But now I'm telling you she's breathing again." Jade turned back into the bedroom, Gander hurrying after. The two men stood looking down at her. The coat lay on the bed, spread away from her body.

"You opened up her coat," Gander said.

"I know. Took a little peek. That's how I saw. Watch."

Her nude body lay lifeless on the mattress.

"I'm watching."

"Look!"

"I don't believe it," Gander said. "She breathed."

"I told you."

Gander swung around to face Jade. "You came in here and opened up her coat just to *look* at her." His fists on his hips. "She was *dead.*"

Jade stared back at him. "Hey, I was just looking. No harm done. So I'm looking and what happens?"

Gander glared at him.

"Her nipples get erect."

Gander glanced down at Patty's breasts. Her nipples stood up like little buttons. He looked back at Jade. "That can maybe happen to a body even if it's dead."

"Oh, I don't think so."

"But why not? If it wasn't dead a long time?"

"But she wasn't dead. Because right then I saw her chest expand. She was breathing."

They watched together, waiting for the next breath.

"What's going on here, Jade?"

"They must've drugged her. I heard about it once. I just never saw it. It's one of the drugs coming out of High Water. They call it Meredith."

"Meredith."

"Yeah. Merry Death. She'll come around, I suppose."

"How long though?"

"Search me."

They surveyed her body.

"You cleaned her up nicely," Gander observed.

"Thanks."

"There's still a little spot, though. At the edge of her mouth? A little red fleck?"

Jade was closer to her face. He licked his finger, leaned down, and ran it along the edge of her lower lip.

Gander asked, "How did you get her mouth to close over her teeth like that?"

"It just did. But I couldn't get all the blood off the teeth yet. I got distracted."

"What did you do with it?"

"With what?"

"The piece of my ear."

"Oh. I flushed it down the toilet."

"You flushed my ear down the toilet?"

Jade smiled back. "What did you *want* me to do? Save it and glue it back on?"

"I don't know," Gander wondered. "It was my ear."

Jade's smile gave way to foolish grinning. "Maybe we could've *buried* it," he suggested, the grinning dissolving into laughter, Jade losing himself and interrupting everything he was trying to say: "You know. A quiet service. Just a few close friends." Laughing with sore cheeks. "Put it on a charm bracelet. Here, honey, for you. Or maybe stick it under your pillow for the earlobe fairy!"

"Oh, you're funny. Sooo funny."

Jade stopped short, swallowing. "She's *awake*."

Patty's eyes were wide, dark, and shining, and staring at the two men standing over her.

"Patty?" Gander asked.

She stared back without answering.

"Patty?" he repeated. Again no answer.

"What the hell am I going to say to the cops?" Jade whispered into Gander's ear.

"Do you think she can hear us?" Gander whispered back.

"Damned if I know."

"Patty?" Gander said. "Patty?"

"Hi, Harvey."

He knelt beside her. "Patty." Looking into her eyes, he reached down for her hand, but his fingers closed instead on the small tuft of hair between her legs. He glanced down, found her hand and held it gently. "Sorry," he said. A slow smile spread across her face. Jade snorted.

"Jade," Gander said without looking back, "why don't you go call the cops or something?"

"Too late. On their way."

"Patty, are you all right?"

"I feel wonderful."

"You do."

"What happened?" she asked.

"We're not sure. We came back and found you."

"She doesn't seem real concerned," Jade observed.

"Jade," Gander answered.

"Yeah?"

"Never mind," Gander concluded and reached across Patty to draw the beige raincoat over her. "Patty, can you walk?"

"I feel wonderful."

"Yeah, I know. Let's try walking."

He held her hands and drew her to a sitting position beside him on the bed.

"It's all right?" he asked.

She lay her head on his shoulder and looked up through her lashes. "I just feel wonderful."

They sat together on the bed, Jade standing before them. "You know," he said, "this is quite a picture. This Meredith stuff is sort of interesting."

"What are you going to tell the cops?"

"She was in a very deep sleep," Jade considered. "Period."

"And you mistook her for dead?"

"I have no idea what I'm going to tell them," Jade admitted.

"You thought I was dead?" Patty asked.

"Not for a minute, honey," Jade assured her. "Tell us what's the last thing you remember."

Patty looked up smiling at Jade. "I was with Harvey." She looked at Gander. "Harvey? Do you think I could have a glass of water? I have this *taste* in my mouth."

"Jade. Get her some water."

Jade shrugged. "Sure, but maybe she should brush her teeth or something."

Harvey and Patty sat together on the sofa, Jade opposite them, the whiskey bottle propped on his knee. "We might think about getting out of here before the cops come."

Gander looked at Patty. "You and I should go somewhere," he said. He looked over at Jade. "Patty and I should head out of town, go hide out somewhere."

"No way, partner. You and I are sticking together for a while."

"Waves of joy," Gander said.

"I was thinking maybe about a hotel," Jade said.

"What about the Grand?" Gander suggested.

"Too obvious. Something more out of the way. There's a place down in the Southern Tier. The Marlin Arms."

"A marlin is a fish," Gander said. "Marlins don't have arms."

"It's not too fancy," Jade allowed. "But it's a place to lie low and get some sleep."

"I like it," said Patty.

"I'm so tired," Gander said.

"Me too," Patty agreed, laying her head on his shoulder.

In a dark and idling taxicab Harvey and Patty waited outside the front entrance of the Marlin Arms.

"He's taking so long," Patty said. She sat curled on the seat next to Gander, her hand under his arm. "It's *cold*."

Gander slid his arm around her. "Is it wearing off?" he asked.

She nodded. Her knee rested against his leg. She nestled her face against his shoulder.

Tapping at the glass.

Gander rolled down the window. "Where've you been?" he said.

"They've only got one room," Jade explained, leaning down. "It's got two beds, though."

"I thought this was some out-of-the-way place nobody'd ever heard of."

"I guess they heard about it. The guy inside said more rooms'll open up when people start checking out in the morning."

"Jade, why don't you just go home?"

"I wanna keep an eye on you."

Gander started to speak. He gave up. He was too tired to argue.

• • •

They stood in the open doorway, looking in at the room. It was brown and slightly larger than the two double beds. A narrow bedside table with a lamp separated the beds. Overhead, a single ceiling light burned brightly.

"It's a room," said Jade.

"It's a room at the Marlin Arms," Gander corrected.

Patty walked in and sidled down the end of the first bed and up the middle to the lamp. "It just needs better light," she encouraged, leaning down and turning on the lamp. Jade flicked off the overhead switch.

"See?" she said.

"It's a room," Jade said.

"A room at the Marlin Arms."

"It's too late," Gander complained. He lay on the bed next to the bathroom door, which was also the bed nearest to the hall door. Jade sat at the foot of the other bed, which was next to everything else. Patty was behind the closed bathroom door with the water running.

Jade said, "It's a quarter to five."

"My head hurts."

The water stopped. The bathroom door opened and Patty edged around it. "There's not a whole lot of room in there," she said. She wore two white towels, one around her waist, the other under her arms and across her chest. "These towels are so teeny," she said, "but I *refuse* to wear that awful coat another minute. It gives me the creeps."

Gander and Jade both stared at her without speaking. The towel around her waist split up her right leg, her bottom visible and curving up and away under the cloth. The upper towel fell across her breasts and then down and just stopped, hanging away from her body, her midriff bare. "Move over, Harvey," she said. She reached for the edge of the bed linens, lifted them, and scooted underneath, her head propping up on the pillow and looking out. "You guys make me feel like I've got nothing *on*. It's not like you haven't seen me without my clothes about ten times tonight."

"That's true," Gander acknowledged, looking at Jade, and Jade answered, "That's true," and they turned back to Patty, nodding.

She burst out laughing and yanked the sheet over her head, laughing and shaking. She stopped and peered out over the edge. "Aren't you guys going to sleep?" She tossed back the corner of the sheet for Harvey. Her whole face shone. "Here," she said, "I'll turn off the light." She reached across to the lamp, the upper towel falling away as the room went dark. Gander stripped to his shorts, piling his clothes on the floor beside the bed. He climbed in beside her. She moved instantly against him, her lips almost touching his ear, whispering so quietly it sounded like a voice inside his head: "Tomorrow, when he goes, we can stay here."

They listened as Jade undressed in the dark and climbed into his own bed.

"It feels so good to lie down," Patty said. "Good night, you two."

The room was silent and black.

Gander staring at the ceiling.

The Marlin Arms

He sat up, breathing noisily.

Patty was gone. Jade was gone, the little room bright and empty.

He pushed himself to the edge of the bed and stood.

"Oh, man," he said.

He stepped into the dark bathroom and stood at the toilet, washed his hands at the sink and splashed his face, rinsed his mouth and combed his hair with wet fingers, and only then flicked on the light and looked into the mirror: unshaven, pale, worn at the eyes, bloodshot and bandaged. He turned the left side of his face toward the mirror. A stain on the bandage marked his ear, a small red country on a white map. He gently lifted the edge to look. He laid it back down and smiled weakly at the disconcerted face looking back, then flicked off the switch.

Leaning back against the pillows, he watched the ceiling, sunlight pouring through the window. Scattered motes of dust floated in the glare. He wondered. What would it look like when it healed? Although he had seen it now. He pretty much knew. The ragged edge of some foreign country.

This is where the voice-over starts, he thought. In the movies, when it's all over but everyone is still waiting and the narrator is looking back and explaining that it's possible to survive the most preposterous odds, move on, and, years later with a wife and three kids, tell the story when they gather around, when they look up at you, when they suggest that, if you do have to go out, could you maybe wear your hat angled a bit to the left so as not to make it so *obvious?*

Gander turned to face the window, staring into the sunshine. Behind him a key slid into the lock. The knob turned and the door opened.

"You're awake."

He turned to see her.

"Patty," he said.

She wore the beige raincoat and carried a small brown grocery bag. "I'm so glad you're awake," she said, coming over to the bed. She sat on the edge next to Gander and leaned over, laying a hand on his cheek. "How does it feel?"

"It feels good to see you."

"You tossed in your sleep." She held his hand. "Here," she said, turning to her bag, "I've brought some coffee. I hope you like it with milk."

"Milk's fine. I kept you awake?"

"Not really. I was too tired. But you must have been dreaming. There's sugar if you want."

"Just the milk, thanks. I don't remember a thing."

"It's probably just as well. I bought some rolls, too. You should eat something."

"I'll start with the coffee."

"Harvey, would you mind very much? Could I ask you a favor?"

"Patty, just ask."

"Would you mind if I wore your shirt?" She looked down at the raincoat. "It's this *coat*," she said, looking dismayed.

"Patty."

She raised her eyes.

"Put on the shirt."

She looked out just before closing the bathroom door. "And I'm going to change that bandage, too."

They lay together on the bed, leaning against their separate pillows, sipping their coffee.

"Better?" she asked.

"A little," he said, then glanced over. "How are *you* feeling?"

"So funny. And a little light-headed, but otherwise all right. Whatever it was they gave me really sent me."

"Do you remember any of it?"

"At your place when I woke up, but not before."

"Nothing?"

"I remember everything about *that*," she said, sliding closer. She leaned forward slightly and he slid his arm beneath her, his lips brushing her hair.

"This morning when I woke up," he said, "I felt like the last person on earth."

"I want to stay with you here all day."

"At the Marlin Arms."

"At the Marlin Arms where we've got everything in the world we could possibly need."

Gander waited, but he said, "I have to go out. I'm sorry, Patty, I have to."

"But why?"

"I have to see someone."

"Who? Natasha Nyle?"

"Definitely not Natasha Nyle."

"Sorry. Just checking."

He kissed her cheek.

She looked up at Gander and burst into a brilliant smile.

. . .

The ceiling light coated the bathroom in yellow glaze. Gander sat
in his boxers on the toilet lid, a white towel spread across his shoulders. His T-shirt hung from a towel rack. A white washcloth
floated in warm water in the sink.

Patty stood over him, one hand curved behind his head, holding
it in place, the other pouring a glass of water, one warm dollop at
a time, behind the bandage covering his wounded ear. Dried blood
dissolved in the slow running water and dripped down his neck
into the white towel, staining it rust.

"Here we go," Patty said, pulling at the bandage with two fingers. "It's coming away." She unwound the white cloth from his
head and stepped back. The bandage hung down from her hand,
reaching toward the floor.

"Say something," Gander said. "You're making me nervous."

"You saw it?" Patty said.

"I just want you to say it's not so bad."

"And here I am just staring at it," Patty answered. "I'm sorry."
But she kept staring at the ear, the oddly serrated wound. She
turned Gander's head in her hands for a better look, saying abso-
lutely nothing.

Gander's voice rose: "Pat-*ty*."

"I'm thinking, I'm thinking."

"And?"

"I can't believe he bit your ear."

Gander met her eyes. "Me either," he said.

They lay side by side against the pillows, Gander in his trousers
and a new white bandage that angled around his head like a hat-
band without a hat. Patty smoothed the skirt of Gander's white
shirt across the top of her legs, her long legs stretching away down
the bed.

"You have pretty legs," Gander said.

She didn't answer. She turned a shirt button between her finger and thumb. "Who do you have to go see?" she asked, not looking up.

"York."

"Why?"

"Because he gave me this story. Because when he gave me the story he must've known something he didn't tell me."

"But why *today*?"

"I have to. I have to stop thinking about it."

He stood at the foot of the bed. Patty leaned down into her pillow.

"I feel like a prisoner in this place," she said, but she pushed herself up to the edge of the bed, her bare feet flat on the old green carpet. "I have to tell you something, Harvey."

He sat down next to her, leaning forward to hang a towel on the bathroom doorknob. "I'll be back," he promised.

"It's not that," she answered. "It's about York. Yesterday after you asked me to look in his files, I never got a chance to tell you."

"I forgot. You saw his files?"

"Just for a minute. His files are endless, and I never did find anything on the rescues. But there was a file with your name on it."

"*My* name."

"It was in with the files on the Superlative Man," Patty explained, "although it wasn't really about you. It was a story about your parents. I just never knew that about them, Harvey. I never knew the Superlative Man practically killed them. I'm so terribly sorry. No one ever told me."

Gander stared at the wall.

"What is it?" she asked.

"The story about my parents. What's it doing in with the files on the Superlative Man?"

"Harvey, it's a story *about* the Superlative Man."

"That file has *my* name on it. It's about me."

"But it gets *filed* under the Superlative Man. Let's face it, Harvey. As far as the world is concerned, it's not a story about you."

"It's as though the rest of us don't even matter," Gander rued.

Patty watched him. "I'm starting to wonder," she said.

"About what?"

"Did York give you the assignment to write about the Superlative Man because of what happened to your parents?"

"I hope not," Gander answered. "I really hope not. But maybe York is deeper into this than I thought."

"Harvey, if it's true, you shouldn't be going to see him today. You're in no shape for this."

"I have to, Patty. I have to find out."

Paul York

He stood on the curb watching cars pull away in the afternoon traffic. It was after four-thirty and the rush hour hardened the city's arteries. Traffic squeezed by at a crawl. A cabbie caught his eye through an open front window, and Gander considered walking the fifteen blocks to the *Metropolitan Meteor*, then thought better of it and climbed into the back to join the slow stream. But he sat back against the smooth black seat for three or four blocks, watching people rise into view and fade, all the hats and skirts, the lipstick and beards, pictures blurring one into the next, and he'd passed Fifty-sixth Street, Fifty-fourth, held the overhead strap as they rounded the corner onto Concord, the Oceanic Power and American Light Building towering beside, before he took a good hard look into the front of the cab, studying the driver's face in profile for the first time. The driver's eyes waited in the rearview mirror, staring back, the edge of his mouth drifting into a smile.

Gander leaned forward. "Turn this way a second," he said. The driver obliged, looking back over his shoulder, smiling in recognition. Gander sat back against the seat. Neither man spoke. The driver drove and the rider rode, until at length Gander broke the impasse.

"You're working a double shift," he suggested.

"Sometimes," the driver answered.

"It was you, wasn't it?"

The smile.

"You've been driving ever since you let me off last night?"

"This morning," the driver corrected. "Off and on."

Forty-ninth Street. The big iron statue in front of the Elephant Theater and its vaulted roof.

Gander spoke to the window beside him. "Tell me something," he said. "How many taxicabs would you say are in this town?"

"Oh, thousands."

"That's what I would have said."

American Airways. The Metropolitan Hotel. The *Daily Mercury*. Club Pair o' Dice. All the passing places.

"And how many people take cabs? In a single day. Just as a guess."

"Oh, tens of thousands."

"Yeah. That's about what I would have said."

"I know what you're going to say," the driver tossed over his shoulder.

"Who me?" Gander answered, the crowded sidewalk drifting by. "Not a chance," he said.

They turned onto Market, the *Metropolitan Meteor* rising ahead.

"Go all the way to the end of the next block," Gander instructed. "Go through the light and let me off at the opposite corner."

The driver protested. "You said you wanted to go to the *Meteor*."

"Right. Now I'm saying something else."

"Okay, okay."

At the curb beyond the streetlight, Gander climbed out and paid the driver through the front window. The driver collected the money, made change, opened a logbook, and settled in to wait. Gander leaned against the wall of a building. He lit a cigarette and looked at his watch. Five to five. Then one minute to five. Somewhere a bell tolled the hour. A police car appeared in the intersection, pulling up beside the cab. The driver glanced over at Gander, muttered something Gander couldn't hear, and pulled away into traffic, Gander watching him go. He ground out his cigarette on the sidewalk, the cab rounding the next corner, and headed back toward his office. Even if the cabbie could lay odds Gander would head back there after all, he wouldn't be sure.

Avoiding the main doors, Gander walked down an alley to the delivery entrance. At the freight elevator an old man with a three-day salt-and-pepper beard greeted him, a cap perched on the back of his head.

"Hey, Mr. Gander. Nice to see ya."

"Hey, Otis."

Otis closed the elevator door, cranked a handle, and the elevator lifted to a chorus of aching cables and gears.

"Otis."

"Yeah, Mr. Gander."

"You get caught, they'll can you."

"I don't know what you're talkin' about."

"The whole car's boozy."

"Aw, that. I ain't had but one or two for lunch."

"What are you drinking?"

"What *was* I drinking," Otis corrected.

"Scotch, I'll bet."

Otis turned to face him. "It's that bad?"

"I'm not lighting any matches."

"I need some coffee beans."

Gander nodded. "Tell you what. Give me a shot. I'll owe you one."

Otis grinned and spoke quietly to himself. He lifted a battered gray flask from an inside pocket and offered it, Gander tilting the flask at his lips, sipping the whiskey, then turning and spitting it into the corner.

When the elevator clattered open, the two men exchanged looks. Otis winked, and the door between them closed. Gander stood alone in an empty freight area, the elevator groaning as it descended back into the building.

He pushed through a pair of windowless service doors into a brown tiled hallway stretching the length of the building. Paul York's office sat just around the far corner, and Gander headed toward it, walking past the open doors of a long string of editorial offices. Rounding the corner, he could see York at his desk, inside his glass aquarium with the blue curtain pulled to one side, a plain wooden door wedged wide. He looked up as Gander entered, his hand reaching automatically for the phone. But apparently he thought better of it, his hand withdrawing to the desk's edge, Gander already sitting in one of two chairs facing him.

"Well, well," York said. "Look who's finally here. I've been looking all over for you, Gander. We need to talk. But I was just about to make a telephone call, so if you'll excuse me for a minute, I'll be with you." The master of the moment. In his uniform of fine blue cloth, his silk lining.

Gander sat back and lit a cigarette, dropping the smoking match into a clean ashtray on the desk, studying Paul York.

"Close the door behind you on your way out," York requested.

"You don't need to call anyone, York."

"Excuse me?"

"One of your boys gave me a lift over. Some hack. You don't need to tell anybody I'm here."

"I don't have the slightest idea what you're talking about, but I smell alcohol."

"I just had a drink," Gander acknowledged.

"You look like you've been drinking for a week. As a matter of fact, you look like hell."

"No, just sore. My head hurts every time I lean to the left."

York studied Gander's face, the white bandage, the small red spot at his left ear.

"I don't know what you've been doing to yourself," he continued, cautious now, "but you should get that dressing changed. You're bleeding."

"I haven't been doing anything to myself, York. One of your friends did it for me."

"One of *my* friends! Look, Gander, that's twice. I don't know what you're driving at, but I don't like your tone."

"I notice you forgot about your urgent phone call."

"What is it you want?"

"I heard you wanted to see me," Gander said.

York picked up a black leather cigarette case from his desk and removed a cigarette. "You're leaving yourself open to reprimand, Gander," he said evenly. "Drunk, disheveled, verbally abusive. You want me to go on?"

"No, I'll commit suicide."

"Very funny." York lit the cigarette with an ivory lighter and exhaled away from his shirtfront. "But it's true. I do want to talk to you. I want you off the story."

"I've grown kind of attached to it."

"Well, I'm sorry about that, but I've had to reconsider. I don't think it's time for another Superlative Man series. For a lot of reasons. You can settle for editorial discretion for all you have to say about it."

"I have plenty to say. Why did you assign me the story?"

"I thought you were due."

"You're lying. I found out about the phony rescues."

York waited. Then, "Gander, I don't have the slightest idea what you're talking about."

"Fair enough. Did Karl tell you to give me the story? Or was it the Sultan?"

York's eyes narrowed. "I don't know what you've gotten yourself into, Gander, but you get one thing straight. I have nothing to do with those people. I don't even know them. I do know, however, that they are trouble. Trouble for you, trouble for me, and trouble for this paper. I won't risk it. I want you off the story."

Gander sat back. "You didn't know?"

"I'm telling you."

"Then why did you give me the assignment?"

York paused, but said, "It was Martin," as though confessing.

"Pardon?"

"Before he died, Martin told me something wasn't right about the overdoses. He knew drugs were coming out of High Water, but he thought there might be some deeper source. He asked me to think about giving the story to you if anything ever happened to him. I thought it was a little strange, but a week later he had his heart attack."

"He didn't say why I should get the story?"

"No, but he always kept an eye out for you. He felt pretty badly about what happened to your folks. And I thought, why not? But, Gander, it's turned into something more than I bargained for."

"York, how much do you know?"

"All I know is what I hear, and what I hear is that they killed a girl named Violet Hayes after she talked to you. I can't risk it, Gander. I can't risk my position at this paper. This story is too dangerous."

"You're not taking me off it."

"Gander, you *are* off it. Period."

"No, York. This is my story. It's *about* me. Martin knew that. He knew." Gander stood up, his eyes still on York's.

"Where do you think you're going?" York challenged.

"I'm going back to work."

"I'm warning you, Gander."

"York, look at me. No, *look* at me. I quit."

"You can't quit."

"Too late. I just did."

Gander turned and walked out of the room, York staring after him.

The long empty corridor stretched back to the freight elevator. Halfway down it Gander slowed, watching the double doors. One of them was open a few inches. Stairways and exits flashed in his mind. A hand appeared on the door's edge, pushing it wide, a face following, peering out under the low brim of a hat.

Elmo Jade.

Under the Great Bridge

They stood in the alley outside the freight entrance. Gander leaned back against a brick wall and Jade faced him, taller, leaner, stooping slightly, his hat pushed back from his forehead. They had ridden down with Otis in silence, Gander shaking his head at Otis's inquisitive look.

"Patty said I'd find you here," Jade explained.

"She's at that lousy hotel all by herself," Gander answered.

"She's all right. How about you?"

"I just quit my job."

"Why'd you do that?"

"I went in there to see him because I thought he might be behind all this."

"York?"

"Yeah, but he doesn't have a clue."

"Not about High Water, he doesn't."

"How come you know so much, Jade?"

"I have to. It's my business."

"But why haven't you told me any of it?"

"You didn't have to."

"I thought you were working for them."

"I'm just a reporter," Jade answered. "I chase after stories. Every once in a while one of them chases after me."

"Maybe it's time you told me about this one."

"You know something, Gander?" Jade looked down the alley. "When York first got you into this, I wrote you off." He looked back at Gander. "But maybe you're a reporter after all."

"Then initiate me."

Jade smiled. He looked tired. "Let's get out of here first. Knowing these guys, we're probably being watched."

They walked away from Market Street to the far end of the alley, turned west on Alsop and dropped into a subway station on a north-south line. They followed an underground passage to a sister station a block away, also a north-south line but with connections to the Outer Borough, and from there rode north on a crowded train into a low end of town. They climbed back to the street about half a mile from the Great Bridge and walked two blocks east before Jade hailed a gypsy cab. They continued east until they reached a city maintenance causeway that ran beside the river. The gypsy drifted into a three-point turn and disappeared back into town, Gander and Jade walking along the causeway toward the massive stone pilings under the Great Bridge.

"Jade, where are we going?"

"Up to the bridge."

"I know, but *why*?"

"I want you to see something. They're going to do another double rescue, and I thought you'd like to be here."

"Tonight?"

"Right here over the river."

They stopped at the base of the stone tower rising up into the infrastructure of the Great Bridge. Jade leaned against the foundation, Gander staring out at the river. For a long time neither spoke. Then Gander broke the silence with an angry, chantlike litany: "You lied to me, you pulled a gun on me, you told me to keep doing the interviews."

"I don't think I ever lied to you, Gander."

"You did. You lied about Dime."

"No. I just told you to forget about him."

"It fits into a pattern just the same," Gander said stubbornly.

"What pattern?"

"You keeping me in the dark."

"That's all it was. There were some things you were better off not knowing."

"But you told me to go ahead with the interviews. Back in the coffee shop. You sent me out there. 'Atta boy, Harv, just keep plugging away.' Jade, these people are killers."

Jade turned his shoulder into the gray stone wall and faced Gander squarely. "I don't blame you for feeling double-crossed," he conceded. "But as opportunities go, you were hard to pass up."

"That's exactly what I mean. You used me just to stir things up. Dime could have killed me."

The current moved fast under the bridge. A tugboat on the river fought it, but it wasn't doing much better than huffing in place.

"If it makes you feel any better, Gander, I killed Dime. Last night after you called, I went out to find you and ended up tailing him. I shot him through a plate-glass window. But I figured the less you knew the better if the police started asking questions."

A seagull walked up close to their feet looking for food, cocked its head and eyed them. It flew abruptly over the river.

Jade offered Gander a cigarette. He said, "So I have this little problem. I killed a man last night."

Gander watched the seagull disappear downriver. "Why was he following me?"

"Dime got carried away. But they had a problem all along after

Paul York gave you the stories. They did *not* want you around. Karl and those guys, they were hoping you'd just give up and go away. They let the interviews go ahead, but only with the understanding no one was to tell you anything. When that didn't work, Karl put out orders to scare you off. Then Milo hit you in the face with his pistol and last night Dime about killed you. Ever since you got the story, they've been losing control."

"Did you know Martin told York to give me the story?"

"Yeah?" Jade looked interested. "I wondered about that. But I gather York changed his mind when he heard about Violet. He suddenly realized that this little story maybe wasn't so little after all, and maybe he shouldn't have given it to you."

"That maybe this is News?" Gander said.

Jade nodded. "York doesn't have a clue what this story is really about."

"I'm not so sure I do, either."

"More and more, Gander, it looks like it's about you."

"Keep talking," Gander said.

"When you walked into High Water the other night and hooked up with Violet, they got nervous. You see, to Karl and his boys down at High Water, you're a man with a mission."

"To get the story?"

"It's more than that. The way they see it, you're totally disillusioned with the Superlative Man because of what happened to your parents. They thought Martin's obituary was your first move, and that picking up on Martin's story was your second. They panicked."

"Is that when they killed Violet?"

Jade watched Gander. "Karl's number-one fear is that people will find out what's really going on down there."

"Selling drugs?" Gander asked.

"You wouldn't believe how much money they're making."

"They who?"

"Karl, mostly."

"I thought the place belonged to the Sultan."

"The Sultan still runs it, but Karl took over the distribution. They have a little arrangement. The Sultan gets his rescues and Karl gets all the money he wants."

"I don't get it," Gander said. "What's with the Sultan's rescues?"

Jade didn't answer. The tugboat hadn't moved five feet upriver the whole time they talked. A sailor sat at the stern smoking a cigar.

"Jade, talk to me. Who *is* this guy?"

"He owns High Water."

Gander sat on the river's edge, his feet dangling over the water. Jade leaned against the gray stone piling.

"He makes the stuff," Jade offered.

"So I hear. In his Harem."

Jade studied the back of his head. "Where did you hear that?"

"I heard it."

Jade shrugged. "The Sultan has a knack for it. They say this Meredith is pretty powerful, makes them all feel like the Superlative Man. It hooks them right and left." Cigarette smoke rose along the edge of the gray stone and melted over the water.

"And the Superlative Man?" Gander said to the river.

"What about him?"

"Does he know the rescues are staged?"

"He does, Gander. He knows."

"Jade, what the hell's going on?"

"You have to trust me on this one," Jade answered, gesturing at Gander's back. "The Superlative Man's as trapped by all this as the rest of them. My dream right now is to free him." He crouched on his heels beside Gander, speaking to the side of Gander's face.

"I mean it. I *dream* about this at night. But nobody knows where the Sultan makes his drugs. I've been looking everywhere, but I come up empty."

"The Harem."

"The Harem. Nothing's going to change as long as the Sultan has his source."

Gander climbed up from the river's edge, leaving Jade crouched in profile beside the water. He brushed his palms against his pants. "I know where it is," he said, standing on the roadway, looking down at Jade.

A fish jumped on the river.

"You know where what is?" Jade said, watching the spreading circles on the water's surface.

"The Harem. I know where it is."

Jade stood slowly, his eyes fastened on Gander's. Gander waited, the smoke hot in his nose, then flicked his cigarette into the river. A fish popped the surface and the cigarette disappeared under the blast of the tugboat's horn.

"I don't know whether to trust you or not," Gander said finally. "You're still holding back."

"I've told you plenty."

"I'm not so sure," Gander answered and turned back to the river. He gestured at it with a loose hand. "It's in an old casket warehouse way down the river, about five blocks south of High Water."

The tugboat never seemed to move. It floated under the bridge, smoke pouring from its stack. Jade looked downriver. When he turned back to Gander, he said, "You're something else, you know that?"

"Jade, look."

"Here we go," Jade answered.

Three great hot-air balloons floated high over the Outer Borough, drifting in toward the city, each with a dangling basket hold-ing the tiny figure of a woman. Pastel geometrics decorated the broad, dry sweeps of canvas—sunrise blues and sea-conch pinks, evening lavenders and pistachio greens—rising up to announce on flowing unfurled banners the arrival of Alfonso's New World Air Emporium.

Jade and Gander stood at the river's edge, watching them move out over the water on the far side of the river, twenty stories in the air. Jade touched Gander's shoulder. High atop the Great Bridge, at the stone peak of one of its two great towers, stood the Superlative Man, his cape blowing behind, his arms at his sides, his feet planted wide.

"Here comes the plane," Jade said. "Hear it?"

Gander nodded at the soft drone of an airplane far down the river.

"The pilot's gonna aim it at the bridge," Jade explained. "But watch him eject."

The plane materialized from a black cloud of smoke and, as if on cue, angled sharply down across the sky, a streaking bullet shot directly at the Great Bridge. A small black speck of a man spun away from the diving plane, his red parachute bouncing open and away like a spark.

"Now watch the first balloon," Jade instructed.

High above the river, a small stove firing hot air into the interior of the first balloon exploded upward. Sparks showered down into the dangling nest, and a woman leaned out, her hands gripping the basket, her voice a faraway cry. A lick of flame touched the canvas above her and spread along the candy-glazed surface.

From high atop his tower the Superlative Man sprang toward the speeding fuselage, hurtling across the evening sky, and, as he reached it, he took hold of the plane's tail, seized it in mid-course, and flung it harmlessly to the river below. All along the Great

Bridge people left their cars and moved toward the rail. The Superlative Man spun around and flew toward the burning balloon, drew up short, and floated in midair beside the heavy ropes tying the basket to the flames above. With his bare hands he snapped the ropes, wrapped them tightly in one fist, and carried the woman in her nest, a slow triumphal procession toward the waiting crowds on the Great Bridge.

"Jade, the pilot."

Floating down in his parachute, the pilot watched as the Superlative Man snapped away the ropes and flew away with his prize, leaving behind the burning balloon, like an enormous torch, floating upward and directly into the pilot's path, and raining sparks down upon the remaining two balloons.

All along the railing of the Great Bridge, people pointed and screamed at the Superlative Man, and the Superlative Man smiled and waved with his free hand, until the screaming changed and he turned and saw the pilot, face-to-face with a vast fiery skull, struggling in his harness. The pilot turned in place and, like a man on a down escalator, attempted to walk back up the sky, the flames folding in around him.

The Superlative Man set the basket on the bridge roadway and tore across the intervening chasm, but all along the bridge the people could see that it was too late, as he disappeared into the flames after the burning man.

When a woman in one of the remaining two balloons saw the Superlative Man step into the flames, she lost hope, for her own balloon was now engulfed in fire, hot snatches of canvas raining down, and she leaped from her basket, twenty stories over the water.

The Superlative Man emerged slowly from the fireball and stared at the lone woman survivor, then at the river's littered surface far below, his head tilting back and his voice pouring up the river. He drifted to the side of the last balloonist, lifted her gently from her basket, and floated lifelessly back to the waiting crowds.

Far below, Gander was speaking to Jade: "Jade, that woman. It's Jeannie. It's Jeannie Meere."

The river's surface was dark. Across the way a lavender band floated over the Outer Borough. They walked side by side away from the bridge, heading into the poorest part of town, walking and not speaking. Night had fallen. The city lay in darkness.

Jade finally spoke. "Karl targets neighborhoods like this."

Gander looked up from the pavement at a row of worn and beaten brownstones. "For selling drugs?" he asked.

"Like I said, it makes them all feel like the Superlative Man."

Across the street on a corner, a local bar sat under wide blue letters: The Late Hour. Gander followed Jade in. At the rear of the room, a man poked his long, thin face out through a curtain.

"What'll it be?" he said, walking over to their booth.

"Scotch," said Jade.

Gander asked, "What've you got to eat?"

"Hardboiled eggs," the man answered.

"I'd like a glass of water," Gander requested, "and a hardboiled egg."

Gander peeled his egg, glancing over to watch Jade. "I want to finish this story," he said.

"Meaning?"

"I think I've got one more interview."

"Who?"

"The Sultan."

Jade was quiet a moment. Then he said, "Tonight. I could take you down to High Water."

"He'll be there?"

Jade nodded. "I'll bring you down and get you through the door. After that, it's up to you. You see, I've got plans of my own."

"Do you now."

"Yes, I do."

"Keep me posted, won't you?"

"You'll be the first to know."

They rode a southbound train. Above the empty seats an advertisement asked if they were tired after another long day. Gander turned to Jade, shouting in the roar, "How come you know so much?"

A lone woman at the far end of the car glanced up from her newspaper.

Jade shouted back: "I have two sources."

The train rattled down a crooked stretch of track.

"One's the Sultan," Jade called out.

"You're working for him," answered Gander, shaking his head. "I knew it."

"No," Jade insisted. "I know something no one else knows, so he talks to me." Jade glanced sideways, then leaned closer to Gander and confided, "I know who the Superlative Man is," he said. "He's my other source."

They climbed the stairway from the station to the street. A low black coupe with red lines sailed past under a streetlamp. Half a block away it pulled over to the curb.

"We've been spotted," Jade said.

"Who?"

"Karl. He just drove by."

"Where?"

"Behind us."

They started in the opposite direction, the sidewalk moving under Gander's feet.

"Jade," he said.

Something flashed. A low whistle shot across his brain.

"Jade."

"What is it?"

"I should get the bandage changed." The words elastic, out of sync with his lips.

"Here comes Karl again."

The low black coupe rolled by, picking up speed near the next intersection.

"We shouldn't go to the hotel," Jade said. "They'll know where Patty is."

"I need to sit down."

"All right, we'll head to your place. Hell, I don't know what difference it makes. We're going down there anyway."

In the kitchen Jade unwrapped the bandage. "You should get this checked," he said, studying the ear, parting the hair to peer at the wound at the back of his head.

"Just clean it out."

"Why don't you have a drink first?"

"I don't feel like drinking."

"Then hold your breath."

Gander wore a fresh suit. A new bandage torn from a sheet sat on his head at a jaunty angle, a spot of red marking his ear. The kitten slept on his arm. Jade shuffled cards.

"I'm calling Patty," Gander said. "She's down there all by herself."

"Suit yourself."

"What's that supposed to mean?"

"You're going to make her nervous is all."

"She's been alone in that lousy hotel all day."

"Suit yourself."

Gander sat back down in his chair. Jade shuffled cards.

Gander asked, "Did you mean that you know who the Superlative Man is? Or that you know the Superlative Man?"

Jade stopped shuffling. "Forget the Superlative Man, will you?" He started shuffling.

Gander stared at his coffee mug. He said, "I'm stopping to see Patty on the way to High Water."

"Suit yourself."

"I am. I'm taking the kitten to her."

Jade set the cards on the table. "Okay, okay. We'll stop. But no long visits, you hear?"

"Sure, sure," Gander answered, and then, "Jade?"

"What now?"

"Did they do that thing to her just to scare me?"

"What thing?"

"When they put the piece of my ear in her mouth and laid her out like she was dead."

Jade shook his head. "That's Karl. Karl is something else."

The cards sat on the table.

The Sultan

It was after midnight when Gander walked out the front entrance of the Marlin Arms. Jade sat in the backseat of the cab, staring ahead at the windshield.

"Sorry," Gander said, climbing in.

"It's okay."

"I just wanted to give her the kitten."

"It's okay."

"I'm glad we stopped. She was worried."

Jade looked across at Gander. "It's okay?" he said.

Gander nodded. "It's okay."

The cab rolled into Stage Alley and stopped at the entrance to High Water. They stood on the curb watching it pull away.

Gander said, "I left this place last night at a dead run."

Jade stared at the blinking red sign. "I told you. They're not going after you for that."

"You sound pretty sure."

"I am. Listen to me. You're going to be this miserable night's main attraction, Gander. They'll all be watching you. So be interesting as hell. I have my own work ahead of me, but what I need is a little time, which I get if they're paying more attention to you than they should be.

"Your ear's bleeding again," he added matter-of-factly.

Men and women pressed into the bar, drinking and talking. At the far end of the room people danced in front of an empty stage. Gander listened for music but heard only the low pulse of voices.

They threaded their way through the tables and dancers and entered the hallway at the back of the room. The door to the women's bathroom stood wide, and inside a man and a woman sat on the counter of sinks, facing one another. The woman's shirt was open, her breasts bare, the man attempting their likeness on the mirror with a bar of soap.

They continued down the hall, through the door at the end marked Private. Ahead was the doorway into the janitor's closet. Gander whispered: "Jade, I am *not* going back downstairs in that elevator." Jade looked over his shoulder, shook his head, and pushed through the glass office door that Gander and Milo had passed the night before.

The office inside was nearly dark. A brass lamp lit an empty desk blotter. Beyond it, at the hem of an inner door, a thin red strip of light glowed on the carpet. Jade stood at the door, red light reflecting on his shoes. He knocked three times, paused, knocked twice, paused, knocked once. The door opened a fraction. A strip of a woman's face.

"Yes?" she said.

"Jeannie, it's Jade. With a friend."

"Oh?" the familiar voice escalating, high-pitched, interested. Gander could picture the tiny lines fanning away from her eyes.

"Harvey Gander," said Jade.

Jeannie stepped aside, opening the door, and Gander and Jade stood bathed in red light. But even as they walked inside, Jeannie

making her exclamations of surprise and welcome, Jade was interrupting her, leaning over and speaking into her ear. Jeannie concentrated her attention on the floor, nodded, and, looking up at
Gander, smiled vaguely, Jade muttering excuses and walking away
to the other side of the room where he joined a group of three
men and two women, all turning to greet him. All except a thin
pale woman, standing slightly apart and reminding Gander of Violet Hayes. She was watching Gander.

The men wore evening dress, black ties circling their necks, the
red light dying their white shirts rose. One of the women wore an
off-the-shoulder, floor-length dress that might have been a shade
of red. In the light it took on the color of old blood. The other
woman—the one watching Gander—had on a short black dress
and high black heels, the tiny skirt split high up her thigh.

Jade gestured back suddenly at Gander and the group turned as
one, then turned back to one another, talking as though Gander
and the woman in the short black dress, still staring at Gander,
were not even there.

Jeannie was speaking. "She interests you?"

"Pardon me?"

"You interest her," Jeannie encouraged. "Does she interest you?"

Gander looked into Jeannie's inquisitive face, framed with long,
sparkling earrings and crowned with piles of jet-black hair.

"Not particularly."

"I didn't think so," Jeannie concluded with a small heave of her
bosom.

"Who is she?"

"Meredith," Jeannie imparted. She held her hands together at
her chest and looked intently at Gander. "I've been hearing so
much about you, Harvey," she said. "Wicked gossip."

"Well, that makes two of us, Jeannie, because I've been hearing
a lot about all of you."

"You know how people talk," she confided. Her voice dropped

to a whisper. "Jade tells me you're upset about our friend Violet. Let me tell you, honey, everyone's mighty unhappy about that."

Her voice ran back up the scales. "Can I get you something to drink?"

Gander smiled in spite of himself. "Not this time."

She sighed. "Not even one of my specials?"

Gander shook his head. "You're amazing, Jeannie. You really are."

"Whatever do you mean?"

"You don't have to pretend. I saw the rescue tonight."

She watched him a moment, then turned as though she hadn't heard and started away across the room. Gander interrupted. "Jeannie," he said, loud enough for the room to hear.

She stopped and looked back sideways.

Gander watched her eyes. "I want to see the Sultan."

Jeannie waited, still watching, then said, "Follow me," and turned and disappeared through a curtained doorway at the far end of the room. Gander glanced back at Jade, but followed her through the curtains into a long, high-ceilinged, blue-lit room, which until his eyes adjusted looked slightly purple.

Twenty or thirty people sat or stood in clusters about the room. Across the floor a vine-patterned carpet absorbed their low conversations. Down the walls on both sides, regularly spaced floor-to-ceiling drapery, thick and closed, suggested new hallways or other rooms.

When they first entered the room, every purplish face turned to see. And, like those they'd left behind in the red room, most were dressed for the evening, the men in dark suits or black tie, the women, their hair up and shoulders bare, draped in black or red. But like the gathering in the first room, most of the conversations were punctuated by the lone, overlooked presence of a single woman in a short black dress, staring out across the room, or at the talking others, isolated within the conversation like a piece of furniture, or a pet.

"Don't look so unhappy."

It was Jeannie, at his elbow.

"Why? Do I look unhappy?"

"My point exactly. Why do you look unhappy? Look. There's Natasha. That should cheer you up, Harvey. She has a little crush on you, you know."

Across the room a curtain had parted, Natasha Nyle stepping through to join the tiny congregation before it. Gander turned to Jeannie, but Jeannie was already slipping away, back through the curtains behind them, Jade appearing beside her and sidling by as she left.

"Gander," he whispered as he approached, coming close to Gander's unbandaged ear. "Listen to me. I'm leaving."

"No way," Gander answered. "I'm not leaving until I've seen the Sultan."

"No, *I'm* leaving. You're staying. I'm going down to the laboratory. Everyone's here. The Sultan, Karl, Jeannie, the whole crew. Our timing's perfect."

"Perfect for what?"

"Trust me, Gander."

Gander's eyes narrowed, but before he could turn, Jade's lips pressed briefly against his earlobe.

Jade's voice fell to a hush: "Thanks, Gander. You're something else."

Gander looked squarely into Jade's eyes. "So help me, Jade, if this isn't on the level, I will hunt you down."

Jade's eyes gleamed, but he turned and was gone through the curtains, Gander watching them fold back into place. Behind him Natasha was calling his name, approaching across the carpet in her black high heels, her short black dress.

"Hello, there," he answered.

"I'm glad you're here." Her eyes bright and shining. "I could use a lift. We all could."

The light had faded from slightly purple to pale blue. It was changing again, from pale blue to a soft green. Gander followed the lines of recessed lights along the edge of the floor, around the edge of the ceiling. He could not tell whether they had changed gradually, imperceptibly, or whether they had simply changed. They were green. Everything in the room was bathed in green.

"I saw the rescue," he said.

"It was awful," Natasha admitted. "Everyone is miserable about it."

"Even here in Candy Land?"

Natasha nodded.

"I don't get it, Natasha."

"You don't get what?"

"When you left my apartment, why did you come back here?"

"Oh, Harvey, not you, too. Please." She leaned over to kiss his cheek, but drew back suddenly. Someone had entered the room behind him. He hadn't heard a thing, and no one looked his way. The quiet conversations continued around the room. But something was happening in Natasha's bright eyes.

"You wanted to see me?" a voice behind him spoke.

Gander swung around and they stood face-to-face.

He was six feet tall and wore an immaculate tuxedo, one hand in his pocket, his other hovering in front of his jacket, holding a glass of clear water. Wide, flat, pressed perceptibly, resolutely forward, his face was a puzzle of light and shade, his eyes concealed behind a pair of dark, almost black, sunglasses, a bold stroke sideways across his face, a line of darkness banding two halves in uneasy collusion. Only his strong cheeks and smooth forehead, rising back into oiled black hair, seemed to hold his face together.

Gander's dislike for the man was immediate and intense.

"You've been causing me trouble," the Sultan spoke again.

Gander answered, "Maybe you deserve it."

The Sultan nodded. "Maybe so, but I have to decide what I'm going to do with you."

Gander felt the attention of the room behind him. He said, "That's your problem. I'm not leaving until I find out who killed Violet."

"Forget her."

Gander shook his head. "I'm in this too deep," he answered. "Somebody's trying to pin her murder on me."

"What do you propose to do about it?"

"I'm going to find out who did it. I'm going to get my story."

The Sultan's hand rose to press his glasses more snugly against his face. "Keep at it," he stated, "and the next story could be your own obituary."

Gander's hands drifted into his trouser pockets. "You think I'm just some meddling reporter, don't you?"

"I don't waste time with meddling reporters," the Sultan assured him, leaning over to set his glass on a low end table. He watched Gander. Gander watched his reflection in the black glasses.

"So I hear," Gander said quietly. "Milo told me what you did to Martin Gale."

The Sultan's voice fell suddenly to a whisper. "I had nothing to do with that," he insisted.

"What about Violet?"

"I had nothing to do with her, either. I have nothing to hide here. I did not kill them."

"For a man who has nothing to hide," Gander said, "you're trying awfully hard to scare me away."

The Sultan looked about the room, and Gander turned to see.

The faces stared back, blank and watchful, except for Natasha, standing beside a tall spidery plant. Natasha stared at the carpet. "I never wanted to see you here," the Sultan confessed. "None of it was meant to be this way." The black glasses turned to Gander. "Come with me. We should continue this conversation in private." He started away, but paused and looked back. "I always wondered how we would meet again. I never guessed it would be a day like today."

"I've never seen you before in my life," Gander answered, not moving.

"We need to talk," the Sultan said. "Come with me."

Gander hesitated, glancing back at the curtained doorway, but followed across the vine-covered carpet, through the soft green light. As he walked he felt newly connected to the small gatherings of people around him, an awareness that seemed to double back in their awareness of him, and grow communal. Natasha's face turned slowly toward him. She smiled and turned slowly away.

The Sultan held aside a heavy curtain, his dark glasses flat at Gander, and Gander passed through into a small living room, the drapery falling to a close behind them. A burgundy wing-backed chair faced a black leather sofa, a narrow side table nestled beside it. An Oriental carpet roiled across the floor, red-shaded sconces dotted the four walls, and cold ashes sat heaped on a fireplace grate. Beyond the fireplace, a short vestibule ended at a closed white door.

"Sit there," the Sultan directed, gesturing at the sofa. He assumed his own place in the burgundy chair, placing his hands on the armrests, crossing his legs at his knees, and leaning slightly forward toward Gander. "You pose a problem for me, Mr. Gander," he said. "You've interfered with our work down here."

"I can think of some people you've interfered with, too," Gander answered.

"I told you. I didn't kill them."

"Whether you did it yourself or ordered Karl to do it makes no difference to me."

The Sultan leaned back into the leather cushion. "I have no control over Karl."

"He works for you, doesn't he?"

"He used to. Unfortunately, he's more like a partner now."

"Whatever you say," Gander answered, dismissing the distinction. "All I can tell you is that when I write up Violet's story, it's going to be murder pure and simple."

"Is that all you want? A story?"

"I want to know what happened."

"It's not that easy, Harvey Gander. I wouldn't even know where to begin."

"Why don't you try beginning with the phony rescues."

"The rescues? The rescues were what the people wanted."

"You mean the double rescues last spring?"

"No, those came later."

"What's that supposed to mean?"

"This goes back quite some time."

"How long?"

"Years, I suppose."

"But *how*?" Gander blurted out, and then stared across the carpet at the Sultan's black glasses. "My parents' accident," he said, his thoughts rapid and disjointed. "There was a boy on the bridge who was going to jump." His palms pressed against the sofa cushion. "When the Superlative Man flew in front of my parents' car, there was a boy on the bridge. Was *that* staged?"

The Sultan's head bobbed silently.

Gander stood and reached out his right hand, his right forefinger pointing at the Sultan's face. "Take them off. Take off those glasses."

"I can't."

"Take them off."

The Sultan rose from his chair and watched Gander without speaking. Then he walked heavily across the room to the curtained doorway and pulled a small brass ring in the wall. A door slid across in front of the curtain to close with a click. The Sultan turned a latch, locking it.

"I'm sorry I have to lock us in," he said, crossing back to his chair, "but they don't know." The Sultan sat back down to face Gander, then reached up and pulled the dark glasses away from his face.

The effect was instantaneous.

The face that had seemed a broken patchwork of black and white melded suddenly and gracefully into a whole. The Superlative Man's features magically assembled, the high strong cheekbones and clean contours of his jaw tracing a framework of unquestioning purpose.

Even as Gander marveled at the transformation, he wondered at a familiar sensation overtaking him. Images from earlier sightings flashed in his mind: The Superlative Man streaking across a gray sky, a fleck of red and ivory. The Superlative Man down a side street as Gander passed in a cab. The botched rescue only hours earlier. And then he remembered: *Staring across his parents' open graves, their eyes connecting, Gander feeling the Superlative Man's gaze sink deep within.*

Gander recoiled in distaste. "What have you *done*?" he demanded.

A momentary light flickered in the Superlative Man's eyes, then nothing.

"What are you *doing* here?" Gander insisted.

"These people help me with my rescues," came the answer.

"It was you," Gander said in disgust.

"It was perfect. Until your parents' accident, it all worked perfectly."

"I'm sure it did. Just like the rescue tonight."

"It wasn't supposed to be like this," the Superlative Man mourned.

Gander listened, his mind racing ahead, stumbling on half-truths. He said, "You do this all with some drug you call Meredith."

The Superlative Man looked up, startled. "Where did you hear that?"

Gander pressed on. "You discovered it," he said, "and then you started taking it."

The answer floated back, flat, lifeless: "I was experimenting with chemicals a few years back, trying to find an antidote to a terrible mineral that saps me of my strength. I built an entire laboratory and never could find it. What I did discover, though, were the most amazing narcotics. Fabulous drugs, and I gave them women's names. I called it my harem. And then one day I discovered something completely new and named it Meredith. People take it once and never want to leave. All I ask in return is their help with my rescues."

Gander dismissed the Superlative Man with a wave. "Those people are all *addicts*."

The Superlative Man sank against the chair, his shoulders deflating, his head drifting heavily to one side, his hands withdrawing from the armrests and retreating lifeless to his lap. "You don't know what it's like. The whole city watches every move I make. They *expect* so much from me, and all the while they act so helpless. I can't stand watching them act so helpless. I can't bear their humiliation. Meredith helps. It changes things."

"So you can forget."

"No, no, it changes the way I feel. I don't feel so *alone*. I feel like the person they want me to be. I feel like the *Superlative Man*."

The words hung in the air. Gander spoke softly, "Tell me about Karl."

"Karl is a problem," the Superlative Man admitted, reaching for the dark glasses in his breast pocket.

"Don't," Gander intercepted. "Don't put those on."

"But the light's hurting my eyes."

"It's practically dark in here."

"I'm due for another dose. When it starts to wear off, the light hurts my eyes."

"Leave them off. I want to see you."

"I didn't spot it at first," the Superlative Man continued. "Karl came in here like all the rest of them, but pretty soon he was distributing Meredith outside High Water. The others came after him, so many I can't keep track anymore. I don't know what to do now. He knows so much. He takes care of so much for me."

"The way he took care of Violet and Martin."

"I can't control him anymore. For him it's a business. But without him I couldn't keep it all going. I couldn't keep making Meredith. And I cannot stop taking that drug."

"You can quit," Gander countered.

"No, I can't."

"You have to," Gander insisted.

"I've tried. I can't do it."

Someone knocked softly at the door. Gander swung around.

The Superlative Man called out, "Who's there?"

No one answered, but when Gander looked back, the Superlative Man was wearing the dark glasses. The knocking resumed.

"Karl knows, doesn't he?" Gander said. "He knows who you are."

The face nodded, the corners of the mouth down, frowning, resigned.

Gander left the sofa and knelt before the Superlative Man. "Where is it?" he whispered. "Where do you keep the supply?"

"I only make a little at a time. It just takes a drop. Karl distributes it in sugar cubes."

"Where is it now?" Gander demanded.

The soft knocking resumed again. Or it hadn't stopped. It was there now, a slow insistent beat.

"Look at me. *Look* at me."

The black glasses lifted, staring back.

"It's me. Harvey Gander." And then one slow word after the other. *"You killed my parents."*

The glasses dropped down. "Upstairs," he said into his chest.

"Upstairs?"

The Superlative Man nodded and said, "Through the other door."

"Past the fireplace?"

Again he nodded. "There's an elevator that goes to the top of the building, the one next to the Barnhouse. I have an apartment on the seventeenth floor. I keep it in a bottle, in a humidor beside my chair. Just one bottle. Beside the fireplace."

The knocking louder now. Gander glanced over to the door beyond the fireplace, and then stood, looking down at the Superlative Man slumped in the burgundy wing chair. "Don't move from here," he instructed, "and do not let them in." He walked past the fireplace into the vestibule, opened the door, and, without looking back, disappeared through.

The Superlative Man sat motionless, his hands lifeless beside him.

In an empty basement corridor Gander pressed an elevator button. The door slid open and he walked inside and pressed number 17. A dial over the door rose slowly from the left. It dropped slowly to the right and the door slid away onto an enormous living room.

Across the room a pair of wide glass doors opened onto the night. The elevator door closed behind as he walked out onto a dark green carpet.

The room centered around a heavy wooden desk, bare of papers and holding only a red lamp with a red shade and a spotless green blotter framed in black leather. Beyond the desk the room was empty, a wall of glass looking out over the city. To the left, set in a dark-paneled wall, three logs burned low under a heavy wooden mantel. A single red leather chair faced the fire, a humidor on four thin legs beside it.

On the mantelpiece above the fire sat a little stone man, and Gander took it down from the ledge. He sat back in the red leather chair, staring at it in his hand.

The wooden lid of the humidor beside him was inlaid with pale stars and a crescent moon. He lifted the lid. A green glass bottle with a silver cap lay against green felt.

The small stone carving in one hand, the bottle in the other, he walked out through the open doorway onto a flagstone patio. White wooden furniture lay across stones. A waist-high iron rail edged the terrace. He leaned against it. A warm breeze blew up from the river. The city spread away to the north in a thousand tiny lights. To the south, across vacant lots and empty streets, beyond the gray lattice of a tall chain-link fence, sat the darkened hull of the American Casket Company.

Gander drew back his right arm and hurled the bottle into the night. It traced an arc across the sky, falling above vacant lots. The seconds passed. A small brittle explosion shattered far below. He dropped the little stone man from his left hand into his right, drew back his arm, and froze at the sound of his own name.

"Gander."

He swung around.

Leaning against the door frame, a black silhouette.

"What was that bottle?" Karl asked.

Gander waited, not answering.

"Makes no difference," Karl said. "We can make more. Not that it's gonna matter to you."

"You want me to go," Gander said, "I'll go."

"Yeah, you'll go."

Gander felt something in his right hand and looked down. He was holding the little stone man.

"What's that?" Karl demanded, pushing away, standing straight.

Gander held it out for him to see, and Karl leaned back into the frame. "That's mine," he said. "It's my marker. You know what it means?"

"I've heard," Gander answered.

"It means that's it. You're done. Nice little coincidence, I think."

Something brushed Gander's neck. His fingers lifted to touch it and he looked down. Blood. His ear was bleeding through the bandage. He looked up and his heart beat. Karl stood a foot away.

"You in pain?" Karl said.

"No," Gander answered, retreating, the small of his back touching the rail.

" 'Cause I wouldn't want you to be in pain," Karl said, and his hand shot hard against Gander's wounded ear. White light flashed. Gander's knees sank to the flagstone. On hands and knees, he crawled past Karl's shoes, but felt himself lifted by his jacket collar and dropped back against the rail. He swiveled against it, leaning out, staring at the city.

Far across the vacant lots and empty streets, beyond the chain-link fence, behind the flat black windows of the American Casket Company, a small orange light flickered briefly.

"Elmo," he said.

"Elmo Jade can't help you now," Karl answered. "This is between you and me."

Behind the windows of the deserted factory, an orange flame shot across the ground floor.

Gander turned to look at Karl. "So much for your Harem, Karl."

"What's that?" Karl shot back, shoving him aside. Tiny flames danced behind glass. A window exploded, a small popping noise in the distance. A lick of fire crawled past the broken glass and along the dark bricks. A black truck raced away from the building and slowed at a gate in the chain-link fence, pressed against it and snapped through. On down the line of ground-floor windows, glass panels exploded. Orange light crept behind a second-story window.

Karl screamed: "What *is* this shit?" He seized Gander by the shoulders, hurling him against the railing. *"You're dead!"* he shrieked. *"You're dead, you're dead."*

"Go to hell," Gander answered, and Karl's hand clapped twice against his ear. Gander wobbled and dropped down against the railing, sliding to the flagstone floor, staring up at the sky. Karl's dark figure wavered like a mirage. He reached down and gripped Gander by his shoulders, dragging him to his feet.

Sick with the pain in his head, filled with revulsion for the face he stared into, Gander heard the words like news type across his brain: *I am looking into the face of my own death.* And with a single sweeping movement he reached out and embraced Karl, locked his hands behind Karl's back and, locked together, the two men as one, Gander threw himself backward over the railing, their bodies toppling into the night sky.

Night Sky

He opened his eyes on constellations of stars.

Sitting on the flagstone patio, leaning back on a white reclining chair. Jade sat close beside him, leaning forward in a deck chair. Patty stood with her back to him, leaning against the railing, looking out at the city. Gander pressed his thumb and forefinger against his eyes.

"How long has it been?" he asked.

Patty turned. One arm cradled the kitten against her breast.

"A while," said Jade. "Not too long. How's your head?"

"Oh, fine," the answer.

Patty sat on the edge of Gander's white recliner, hovering over him, the kitten stretching on her leg, arching its back. "Harvey?" she asked, looking into his eyes.

"I think so," he answered, looking into hers.

Jade said, "You never gave me a chance to get back here, Gander. I guess there was a little trouble."

"I remember falling off something," Gander explained, still looking into Patty's eyes. "I seem to remember falling off this building."

"You did fall off this building," Patty said.

"And here I am."

"Here you are," Jade agreed. "The Superlative Man saved you." Jade stood up and walked away into the apartment.

Gander still looked into her eyes. He said, "When did you get here?"

"Just a few minutes ago," she answered. "Elmo called me. He told me what happened. Harvey, I was crazy in that hotel room, I was so worried. They could've killed you."

"You know, it's funny. For a moment up here with Karl, I didn't even care."

She reached for his hand.

When Jade returned, he carried a bottle and three glasses. Gander sat up gently.

"Jade, you set me up. He was waiting for me."

"Go easy," said Jade. "Lie quiet. It's true. I knew he wanted to see you. But I needed to know for sure he'd be at High Water when I went down to the laboratory."

Jade poured two fingers of liquor into each glass.

"I don't want a drink," Gander said.

"I suppose I don't either," Jade admitted. "I guess I just felt like celebrating." He set the bottle and glasses on the flagstone floor.

"I'd like a drink," Patty requested, and Elmo handed her a glass.

"Where's Karl?" Gander asked. "He caught me up here. We went over the side together."

"I know," said Jade.

"Did the Superlative Man save him, too?"

Jade smiled briefly.

Gander stood slowly. "Oh no," he said.

"Sit *down*, Harvey," Patty said.

"She's right, Gander."

"Karl hit my ear," he said. "He kept hitting my ear." Gander shook his head gently.

"You lost some blood," Jade said and nodded at Gander's chest.

He touched his cheek. His fingers traced a line of dried blood down the side of his neck. He stared at his white shirtfront and a wide diamond-shaped stain.

He leaned against the railing. Patty set the kitten on the flagstones and left the recliner to stand beside him. Fire trucks sat scattered around the smoking carcass of the American Casket Company.

"You did it, Jade. You burned it down."

"Couldn't have done it without you, Gander."

Gander looked over his shoulder. "Talk to me. Did the Superlative Man save Karl, too?"

Jade shook his head. "I guess the Superlative Man just couldn't be in two places at the same time, Gander. It was one or the other of you."

Gander turned back to the city. "Then I guess he solved his little problem."

"What little problem?"

"Karl. Where is he now?"

"The Superlative Man? He's downstairs," Jade answered. "He's wearing the scarlet-and-ivory, cape and all, and he's walking around telling everyone it's time to go home. The party's over."

Their eyes met.

"Honest," Jade assured him. "I don't know what happened while I was down at the warehouse, Gander, but you made some kind of an impression."

"It's pathetic, Jade. He's totally addicted."

"I know. He didn't want to be here when you woke up. I think he's afraid of you."

"He needs help."

"You should see him down there, Gander," Jade encouraged, "ordering people to go home, people who've been here for months." Jade leaned back in his chair, his hands clasped behind his head. "Gander, I have to hand it to you. I didn't think you had it in you."

Patty slid her arm through Harvey's. The kitten pressed its two front paws against her ankle. She looked down and knelt to scoop it in her hands.

Stars poked holes in a sky of deep-blue construction paper. A warm breeze blew up from the river and a raft strung with lights sailed down toward the harbor.

At last Jade said, "There's a story in this, you know."

Neither man looked at the other.

"I know," Gander answered. "You write it. You started out long before I came along."

"I thought about that. But then I was talking to a friend of mine down at the *Daily Mercury*, and I told him about you. He wanted to know if you'd come over and work with them."

Gander turned around. "In news!?"

"*Harvey!*" Patty whispered.

Jade nodded. "Here's your first story."